J.E. REED

FERAL MAGIC

THE CHRONOPOINT CHRONICLES

ORIGINS

VOLUME 1: VIXIN

Cover Design: Brosedesignz

FERAL MAGIC

ISBN: 978-0-578-77646-0

Visit the author at jereedbooks.com

Facebook: J.E.Reed.author
Twitter: J_E_Reed_author
Instagram: jereed_kiuno

Also available in ebook

To Mandy—

for teaching me life is meant to be lived.

YOLO.

FERAL MAGIC

1

THE GIRL AND A KNIFE

THREE MONTHS BEFORE KIUNO...

Vixin prowled through the forest with feather-light steps, running her fingertips over the rough tree bark while scanning the vicinity for any signs of life. She'd seen nothing but animals for hours. Animals that weren't as frightened of a human's presence as they should have been.

Her skin prickled as a chilly breeze ruffled her red hair and she resisted the shudder that ran down her spine. Her brows scrunched as she ran her hands over delicate budding leaves and lingered on a thorn. Whatever this place was, it certainly didn't feel like a dream.

She scanned the forest again, running her eyes up and down thick trunks before double checking the foliage beneath. All wrong. Everything about this place was wrong. The bushes. The trees. None of it grew together. Not anywhere in the world she knew anyway. And she knew a lot. Geography was a subject she studied intensely, not only for school purposes, but for survival. One never knew where they could end up. Plane crashes. Train derailments. She'd read all the stories.

Vixin fingered the leaf again. Spring. Early, if she were to guess from the temperature. Her brow furrowed, but that didn't make sense. She'd looked at the calendar last night. January fifteenth. In two days, she was to undertake another test from her father. She'd been waiting for it, preparing for months.

Could he have planned a surprise test instead? Try to make her panic and falter under pressure?

She crouched and glanced toward the bracelet encircling her wrist. A braided leather strap went through a single tan stone. 'Vixin' had been engraved on the surface.

It wasn't her real name, of course, but she'd used it enough times that it didn't bother her to use it now.

Especially since she couldn't recall her own.

Vixin huffed and stood, examining the treetops for what seemed to be the hundredth time. She'd already run her fingers through her hair, searching for a bump that might indicate she'd hit her head. Her father always stopped her tests if she injured herself. That was the only way he'd agree to them. And if she couldn't recall her name, then there was a good chance she'd had some kind of mishap.

But her father wasn't here.

And her father was always there. It didn't matter how difficult the exercise proved. Nor the climate. He never left her unattended.

Which only meant one thing.

This wasn't a training exercise.

Vixin stepped over a twig, careful of her footing. She didn't want to be tracked, and though it was a hard-learned skill, she wasn't about to risk it. If anyone was trying to follow her, they'd have a hard time of it.

She searched the ground, continuing her trek through the woods. Still nothing human, but at least there'd be enough food should she be stuck out here for a few days. Judging from the chill in the air, the nights would be cold, which meant a fire. And a fire could attract unwanted attention.

She'd have to be careful.

Shouting had her falling back, pressing herself against a tree. She waited, counting her breaths as she surveyed her surroundings.

The shouting shifted to screams. Maybe someone had fallen and injured themselves. She didn't particularly care, but at the very least they might have some answers.

Vixin crawled from behind the tree and stalked toward the voice, keeping her steps quiet, her breathing even.

Whimpering followed, and she pressed herself against another tree to examine the scene.

Six lanky men stood over two hunkering figures. Her gaze roamed toward those on the ground, and she noted their bound hands and the scraps over their bodies. One even sported a black eye.

"Please, stop." The black-eyed boy bent his head to the ground. Vixin snorted. She'd die long before she resorted to begging. Her gaze shifted to his bound companion, but his blank stare told her enough. He'd given up, accepted defeat. At least he was willing to take his punishment in silence.

Vixin took to examining the captors, surprised to find them in relatively normal attire. Skinny jeans, poorly dyed hair, and T-shirts with logos she recognized from one band or another. Not men at all. Boys. Bullies.

One flipped a knife in his hand and Vixin turned away. She didn't need to get involved. It wasn't her business. She needed to focus on herself, figure out the situation at hand.

A twig snapped and Vixin cursed. She whirled, her hand reflexively reaching for her hunting knife, but it wrapped around empty air. She took a step back and dropped into a stance. Weapon or no, she could still fight off an attacker.

The young man before her was a bit thicker than his companions, and his hair was greased back with far too much product to label him as a threat. But the way his eyes roamed over her body made her want to cram his teeth down his throat.

He raised his voice rather than lunging for her. "Looks like we have another one."

He inclined his head toward those behind her, an indication to walk. She could have run. Could have easily planted her knee in his groin and sprinted through the woods without worry, but something had her turning toward the other six. Her father would disapprove, but maybe she'd learn something. If not, the fight would at least warm her up.

Upon seeing her, the one with the black eye pleaded. "Help us, please."

The tall one with the knife laughed and pointed the blade toward her. "What do you expect a girl to do? Look at her. She's smaller than I am." Vixin wasn't sure which one she wanted to punch first. Greasy hair or loudmouth. "She couldn't hurt a fly." He licked his lips. "But I bet she screams better than you do."

That caught her attention. Vixin stared him down, taking in his form. Eighteen. Nineteen maybe. All of them seemed about that age, though the boy trying to threaten her looked as though he hadn't eaten in a month. Pale skin, lack of muscle. Yet annoyingly, probably popular among his clique of friends. Such was one of the many reasons her generation annoyed her so. No one knew what to value anymore.

A subtle nod toward his greasy companion sent a thrill of excitement coursing through her body. Vixin spun on her heel as he reached for her. She gripped his wrist, ducked beneath his arm, and wrenched the limb behind his back. He cried out, but not before she kicked his knee in and sent him to the ground. Vixin placed her body on top of his, twisting his wrist as a reminder to keep still if he didn't want it broken.

Loudmouth gaped at her a moment, then tsked and grabbed the young man with a black eye. He pressed the blade to his captive's collarbone. "Let him go or your friend paints the ground."

Vixin couldn't help the giggle that escaped her throat. "Friend? I don't even know who they are." She nodded toward the blade. "And your hold on the knife is wrong." She tilted her head and pointed with her free hand. "It needs to be higher if you plan to slit the artery."

His face tinted and he threw his captive to the ground before lunging for her. Vixin released his companion and stepped back, smirking when her would-be assailant tripped over his ally. Loudmouth scrambled back to his feet and ran at her, swinging wildly. His nostrils flared as he missed time and time again. Vixin smiled at his growing frustration.

He swung a final time, throwing himself off balance, and Vixin shot forward. She gripped his wrist and twisted. He cried out, dropped the blade, and she snatched it from the air before dancing away.

He gaped at her as she twirled the knife between her fingers. "Thanks for this." Vixin grimaced upon examining it. "You could have at least sharpened it."

"You stupid—"

Vixin dashed forward and had him on his knees before he could finish his sentence. She placed the small blade over the rapid pulse in his neck. "This is where the carotid is and with just a tiny flick of the wrist," she moved to add emphasis.

"I'm sorry," he sputtered. His eyes danced between his companions, pleading for them to do something. "We were just playing around, right guys?"

Vixin glanced at the two on the ground and then shoved him forward. "Sure you were." She pocketed the knife and pivoted from the scene. They wouldn't be able to tell her anything useful. In fact, they probably thought this was all some kind of elaborate prank and had no idea dinner wouldn't be served on a silver platter.

"What are you waiting for?" he roared. "Get her!"

Vixin huffed and ducked to avoid—her eyes widened. Was that a sword? She'd just let these bastards off easy and they were going to cut off her head?

She shot her foot out, sweeping her nearest attacker's legs before rolling to place some distance between herself and the other six. What the hell was wrong with them?

Thankfully, only one had a sword and he scrambled to his feet in a way that told her she had nothing to worry about. Playing around indeed. If they were willing to come at her like that—well—they wouldn't be getting off so easy after all.

Five charged at once, two with pitiful weapons, the other three with their fists. Honestly, what group of men attacked a young woman?

Vixin ducked, dodged, and spun around her opponents with ease. She half wondered why her father had bothered training her so hard if this was all she'd have to contend with.

She counted the seconds, knowing exactly when and where their wild swings would strike and how to pivot herself around them so they'd all look like fools.

Her fist collided with the first's jaw followed closely with an elbow to his solar plexus. She slammed her knee into the next one's groin and broke the third's nose with the palm of her hand.

The remaining two faltered, glancing from their friends on the ground to the girl still standing without a scratch.

Vixin walked toward them and they stepped back, creating a wide berth for her to stroll through. She picked up the two knives that had fallen on the ground. Not the best quality, but at least it'd be better than nothing. Vixin stuffed one in her boot and twirled the other between her fingers.

She turned to leave. "Untie us." Vixin tilted her head back to the one with a black eye. He tried struggling to his feet, but failed and she realized they, too, were bound. "Please, just give me a knife."

Vixin huffed and wiped the sheen of sweat from her brow before marching over. Her attackers still hadn't moved, and if they remained where they were, then she wouldn't bother with them. She had more important things to do anyway.

Taking pity on his bound state, Vixin sawed at the ropes binding his wrists, then dropped the knife in the dirt for him to do the rest.

She turned toward loudmouth and could have sworn he'd taken a few steps behind his nearest companion. "If I see you again, I'll be splitting that artery of yours and you'll get to see first-hand exactly how long it takes someone to paint the ground." He swallowed hard and she spun on her heel before stomping away.

2

THE GIRL AND HER MAGIC

Vixin rubbed her temple. Dusk was settling fast, and despite the distance she'd placed between herself and the boys that'd formed that pitiful excuse for a gang, she couldn't shake the two she'd rescued.

They'd been following her for hours, maintaining a safe distance as they strolled through dense foliage and thorns. Vixin purposefully tried taking difficult routes, hoping it might deter their pursuit. Sadly, it didn't.

She glanced toward the setting sun. She couldn't keep going if she planned to make camp, and she hadn't found any clues that might help her solve the mystery at hand.

Vixin stopped and turned with a huff. "What do you want?"

A long pause, then the two approached her carefully. The one with a black eye wrung his hands together, seeming to look everywhere except at her. "We didn't really know where else to go." He gestured at their surroundings. "I thought we could tag along with you?"

"Why?"

Excitement bloomed in his gaze. "Because what you did back there was badass!" When she didn't respond, he cleared his throat and gave her a sheepish smile. "And we don't really know what we're doing."

"So your plan is to use me as a bodyguard? Hate to break it to you, but if we're attacked, I'm not saving your sorry asses."

Fear flickered in his gaze. "We'll put ourselves to use. Do whatever you tell us." He glanced at his companion. "Won't we?" He looked back at her. "Please, just let us tag along. Whatever you need, we'll be happy to do it."

Vixin sighed and pinched the bridge of her nose. She was tired and the thought of having someone do the heavy lifting didn't seem so bad. "Fine. Go gather firewood and if you can manage it, try not to sound like a herd of elephants in the process."

He saluted her. "Yes ma'am." He crashed through the forest, dragging his friend with him. She sighed again. There went her stealth. At least they'd make for good decoys.

Less than twenty minutes later, and with far more noise than should have been humanly possible, the two deposited their third armful of wood at her side. She gave it a sidelong glance.

"I take it neither of you knows how to start a fire?"

"Uh, not really." She huffed and he quickly added. "But I can learn."

"By the time you learn it'll be morning." She headed back into the woods, pulling apart bark and gathering a small pile of twigs. They watched her with the intensity of a cat stalking its prey. Within a few minutes she had a spark, then the fire was roaring. Both looked at her as if she were some kind of alien creature left behind for their amusement.

She poked the fire with a stick, shifting the logs to let it breathe. "Can either of you hunt?" Black eye shook his head. "Find water?" Again, a shake of the head. She huffed again. "Then what good are you to me?"

"We can learn. We're willing to learn." He elbowed his companion. "Right?"

She glanced at the silent boy. Now that she got a good look at him, he seemed younger than the others. Fourteen or fifteen. He still had his head down, hung in defeat and his eyes were red, likely from crying. Vixin turned back to the fire. "Is your friend a mute?"

"Huh? No, he just...isn't sure what to make of all this."

"Did he tell you that?"

"Not in so many words."

"Hey kid." He glanced up at her with amber eyes but didn't hold her gaze. "If you think getting beat up is the worst thing that could happen out here, you're dead wrong. Suck it up, we don't have time for your cry-baby nonsense."

"Hey—"

She interrupted him. "I'm not going to coddle either of you. If he doesn't learn to speak for himself, then he's going to die out here. Plain and simple."

He opened his mouth to argue but changed the topic instead. "Do you know where we are?"

Vixin used one of the knives to pick at her nails. "Not a clue, but I know survival. I know I haven't seen a human track for miles apart from the winners you ran across earlier. I know this place seems strange and I know the animals around here haven't been hunted." She threw another log on the fire. "I don't suppose you know any more than that?"

He shook his head. "Just woke up here this morning and he was by my side." He tilted his head toward the silent one.

"You don't know him?"

"Not really, we just met this morning. Walked a bit then those guys jumped us."

"Why?"

"Said they wanted our money, but neither of us had any, so they started beating us. I don't really get it."

"People like that enjoy making others feel powerless."

"That's terrible."

She shrugged. "It's nothing new."

Silence stretched between them and the fire popped. "I'm Anton by the way." He gestured to his silent companion. "And this is," he hesitated, and Vixin raised a brow. "Well, I've taken to calling him Blitz."

"What?"

Anton scratched the back of his head. "His bracelet says Blitzer."

Vixin let out a roaring laugh. "Blitzer? What kind of name is that?"

"A gamertag," Blitz answered. His voice shook. "It's always been my gamertag."

She stopped laughing. "Gamertag for what?"

He shrugged, pulling his knees into his chest. "For everything."

Her gaze shifted to Anton. "And yours?"

"The same."

Gamertags, what the hell did that mean? She'd dabbled in a few games here and there, but most annoyed the hell out of her so she'd never played long. But she'd also used the name Vixin in an assortment of online forums and learning centers.

Silence filled their little camp again until Anton asked, "Care to share yours?"

"It's Vixin."

"Guess that's better than Blitzer." He tried to laugh, but it was strained, and she didn't return it. How did any of this make sense? Why were they tagged to begin with? Did the bracelets have tracking devices in them?

Vixin examined the small stone and then ran her fingers along the braided leather. Smooth, nothing out of place. She tried to pull it off, but the material seemed just tight enough that it wouldn't fit over her hand. She pulled out her knife and sawed at the leather. Sawed and sawed and sawed, cursing as she tugged and pulled at the material to no avail.

"What the hell are these things made of?"

Anton shrugged. "I couldn't get mine off either." She tugged at it again, but some unseen force kept the bracelet intact and unmarred by her knife. Leather didn't do that. Leather stretched. Leather could be cut. So, what was this?

Vixin finally gave up and stared at the darkness beyond the trees. "It's not important right now anyway." She hoped. What if they were the game? What kind of messed up situation would she have to be in to become the hunted? Sure, human trafficking was a thing nowadays, but did some sicko delight in hunting people for sport?

It still didn't explain why the bracelets wouldn't come off. Indestructible material didn't exist, though her father might have disagreed with her in the moment. Maybe they'd found some—Vixin shook her head. Conspiracy theories weren't going to help. Not right now.

Vixin threw another log into the fire, sending a mass of sparks through the air. She laid back and folded her hands behind her head. She could run through possibilities tomorrow. Right now, all she wanted to do was sleep.

Anton cleared his throat. "Um, Vixin?"

She sighed. "Yes?"

"Do you think you could teach us? How to defend ourselves I mean?"

She didn't open her eyes. "Maybe. If you let me sleep." Vixin heard his little sound of triumph and rolled her eyes. Maybe she'd lose them in the woods tomorrow, disappear behind a tree before they took notice.

Her father's disapproving scowl appeared in her mind. She would have argued with him, but like always, he would have eventually won. Fine, she'd help them, but as soon as she found civilization, they were on their own.

THREE DAYS passed and Vixin seriously considered killing them herself. They complained endlessly. First it was food. Then it was water. Then food again. Then Blitz's feet hurt. On and on and on. If a bear came their way, she'd welcome its ferocity. It'd get Blitz first and Anton would foolishly try to save him while she sprinted away to enjoy her freedom. They reminded her exactly why she didn't mingle with people her own age.

"Need food." Vixin hurled another rock at Anton, successfully hitting him in the shoulder. At least the two idiots gave her good target practice. He hissed and rubbed at the area then glared at her. She glared right back.

"Can you stop doing that?"

"Can you stop complaining?"

"But I'm hungry."

"I don't hear Blitz crying about it."

They continued in silence, passing tree after tree with no end in sight. She knew how large forests could be, but the thought of spending more than a week with two crying fools following her had Vixin wishing she'd been stranded somewhere else. Maybe somewhere she'd be required to kill and eat them.

Vixin grimaced at the thought. Maybe that was going a bit far. Neither had much meat on their bones anyway.

She paused to examine a downed tree, the branches cut and dragged off. Another sat a few paces away, though it had been cut into manageable pieces. Tracks lined the area. Human tracks.

"Finally!" Anton cried.

Vixin fetched a stone from her pocket and hurled it at him, striking the boy in the head. He turned on her, but Vixin placed a finger to her lips and panic covered his face. Both boys mimicked her actions and hunkered behind a tree.

Vixin crept forward until a wall entered her view. A wall that circled around what she could only assume to be a camp. Two armed men stood at the gate, both holding—spears? What was this, the middle ages?

Anton crept up beside her, leaving Blitz to look like a helpless child. Honestly, he probably was, but she wasn't about to pick on the kid anymore. He still hadn't said much, and that made him better company than Anton.

"Why are we hiding?" he whispered.

"Where do you think the boys who attacked you came from?"

His face paled. "I assumed they'd woken up out there like we did."

She raised a brow. "With weapons? Without a care in the world?" She shifted her attention back to the guards. "I'm willing to bet this is their home base and if those are the kind of scoundrels they staff then I'm not walking in announced."

"What are you going to do then?"

Vixin glanced down at her soiled clothes. She hadn't had a bath in days and was sure she smelled just as bad as the boy kneeling beside her. "I don't know about you, but I could use a change of clothes."

Anton's mouth gaped. "Clothes? That's what you're thinking about right now? What about food? Weapons?"

"I suppose they would come in handy too." She gave him a teasing smile, then scooted away from the wall. Blitz and Anton followed and gathered around her. "You two stay here. I'll be back in a few minutes."

Anton protested. "No way, you can't do that by yourself."

"Why, because I'm a girl?" He opened his mouth to respond but seemed to think better of it. "If you tried to come, you might as well make a bullhorn and announce yourself to the world."

"How will we know if you get in trouble?"

Vixin smirked. "I'm always in trouble. That's half the fun, but those guys?" She jerked a thumb behind her. "Amateurs, just like the jerks who attacked you. Trust me, there's nothing to worry about."

WITH THE setting sun, Vixin crawled toward the small village, keeping to the shadows. She kept a careful eye on those patrolling the gate and surrounding area. Okay, maybe she'd lied to Anton a little. They weren't complete amateurs, but they didn't worry her either. She'd crept into enough places to know what to look for. And those usually had cameras.

Vixin's stomach growled, telling her Anton's idea for food might not be such a bad one. She could get it on her own, but that required hunting, and hunting required a weapon. Snares were always an option, but that required her to wait. And she wanted to find out where she was and how to escape as soon as possible.

Vixin ducked behind a trunk as one of the guards turned. She waited, counting the seconds it usually took for someone to dismiss a perceived threat. She peered around the tree then sprinted from her hiding place, jumped to grab the wall, and hauled herself over without making a sound.

She pressed her back against the first house, angling herself into the deepest part of the shadows. A man passed by, looking far sleepier than she thought a guard should. She crept forward and peered into the first window.

Two people slept in a bed together with another four spread out across the floor. Too risky. She scurried toward the next house, swinging around the back to avoid the guard again. But several people occupied that one as well.

Okay, so they weren't in chains. Maybe that group of boys hadn't come from this place. Maybe she could have simply walked through the front gate, dropped off Anton and Blitz, ate a good meal, and been on her way.

But something in her gut warned against it. She didn't know why, could never fully explain it, but her father had told her to listen. He said instinct would keep her alive far longer than any weapon.

Vixin leaned against the third house and crept toward the edge to survey the town's center. Two guards drew her attention, again armed with spears as they stood outside the doors to another house. Either someone important slept there, or they'd just given away the location of their supplies.

Vixin circled around again, sliding along the sides of buildings. She kept one eye on the guards, checking for any shift in body language that would indicate she'd been discovered.

She noted the broken side window. And the shards of glass left in place. They must have left them to prevent any would-be thieves from crawling through. She smiled, checked the guards again, then darted across the short expanse.

Vixin knelt below the window and silently jumped up, locking her fingertips along the edge. She lifted her body, reached beyond the glass, and anchored her hand on the inside before pulling herself through.

She'd seriously have to thank her father for all those grueling workout routines when she returned home.

Vixin scanned the interior. No walls separated the small space into rooms. A few wooden crates sat against either wall, but even these people didn't appear to have much. It made her curious, almost enough to leave and come back in the morning. Almost. That nagging feeling in her gut still told her to steer clear.

She headed straight for the weapon's rack and ran her hands along the dozen or so pieces before settling on a pair of long knives. Vixin examined the edge, running her finger along the surface. Certainly not perfect, but both were far better than the pitiful knife stuffed in her boot.

She opened a crate and rummaged through the leather, finding a set of frogs and a belt that could be slung over her shoulders. She tightened them, creating new holes for the too large buckles, and secured the weapons to her back.

Afterward, it was clothes, most of which proved to be too large on her small frame, but with a few pieces of rope she made them work. Vixin stuffed a few others that she thought might fit Anton and Blitz into a satchel, then reached for the food.

She lifted another lid, but shouts from outside drew her attention. She paused, listening, and then a blaring horn sent her racing for the doorway. Vixin pressed her body against the wall as the door burst open, and she raised her forearms to brace against the swinging impact as a group of men rushed inside.

They tipped the crates, grabbing whatever they could get their hands on. Vixin didn't wait. She slipped through the entrance, but outside had shifted to a very different scene.

Fires lined the area, illuminating all her previous hiding places. Three individuals raced toward the building, each pointing at her, their battle cries echoing through the air.

Cursing her bad luck, Vixin shoved the bag behind her body and drew her new weapons. The first attacker swung, but she dodged to the right, using her blades to block her next attacker. Her foot collided with his shin and she ducked low to sweep his legs from under him.

Something wrapped around Vixin's ankle and yanked her foot out from beneath her. Her elbows stung as she collided with the ground, but whatever had a hold of her began pulling. Vixin spun around, ready to cut herself loose, but the sight made her pause.

She blinked even as her body scooted across the ground. Was it a trick of the light? Were those plants crawling up her leg?

More greenery erupted from the earth like monsters that had a mind of their own. They wrapped around her wrists, pinning her tightly to the ground.

A nightmare. This had to be a nightmare.

Panic flooded her core as a man wearing leather armor stalked forward, more vines connected to his arm. She struggled harder, pulling at her restraints even as thorns bit through her flesh.

He raised his weapon and Vixin yanked harder still. Something deep in her gut responded. She didn't understand it, but somehow, at her desperate command, *things* wriggled beneath the earth and shot out with her desperate cry. They impaled her attacker, and Vixin scrambled to her feet when her bonds slackened.

She stared at his helpless form, blood leaking from the eight holes plants had made in his body. *Plants.* They'd shot straight through his middle, anchoring him to the ground. He let out a strangled cough and then fell still.

Vixin's eyes widened, but the raging chaos surrounding her broke her from the shock. She took a step back, grabbed her weapons from the ground, and sprinted for the trees as fast as her legs could carry her.

Fighting surrounded her, but she sprinted through the gate, her heart pounding. Someone ran beside her, too close for her liking. She cast him a quick glance and they disappeared into the trees together. He eyed her more than once, his arms full of various items while hers only held the daggers. He offered a triumphant smile and Vixin snarled in return.

She refused to stop, her legs pounding in time to her racing heart, but the young man running beside her managed to keep up. Then more people joined. She took a count and slowed her pace, noting that most carried items just as he did. A band of thieves? Maybe this was the group those lanky men hailed from.

With their pursuers so close, she didn't dare stop. With any luck, this group of people would simply think her a new member. Once they were distracted, she'd slip away unnoticed and find the two she'd left behind. With how Anton marched through the forest, anyone would be able to track them down. If they hadn't already been caught.

The one still glancing at her finally slowed to a walk, and she followed suit when others did the same. Two fires illuminated the trees ahead. Vixin glanced to her right, her left, and then behind. A few dozen at least, though it was hard to judge in the dark. Too many eyes to disappear from without notice.

It couldn't quite be called a clearing, but they entered a break in the trees and those carrying items dropped them in a pile at the center. The one who'd run beside her did the same and gave a passing glance to those surrounding the fire. His eyes locked with hers for a brief moment, then passed by. She let out a soft breath.

The young man placed one foot on their small pile of riches and a broad smile crossed his face, but before he could give what she was sure to be a lengthy and embarrassing speech, Anton and Blitz were thrown at his feet. Vixin cursed under her breath.

"We found them lurking on the outskirts of the village."

The one still standing atop their treasures turned to her. "They aren't the only new faces." She bristled, and those surrounding her took several steps back. "Did you follow us to avenge them?"

Vixin glanced around. Fear. Most eyed the weapons still in her grasp. At least they wouldn't put up much of a fight if it came down to it. Her gaze drifted to Anton and the pleading look in his eyes. How did someone manage to become a captive twice in one week? It would be so easy for her to leave them. Get on with her life. Her father's scowl returned.

Vixin sighed and put her blades away. "I have no affiliation with them."

He left his pile, swaggering toward her. "Then what were you doing there?"

Vixin nodded toward the pile of goods. "The same as you it seems."

He looked her up and down, those soft brown eyes betraying the outward confidence he tried to radiate. "Then I guess those belong to us now don't they?" He eyed her daggers and the bag at her side.

Vixin smirked. "Then come get them."

Tension floated between them for a long moment, then he burst out laughing. Caught off guard, her gaze shifted to others in the group who were also snickering, though some did let out a sigh of relief.

He held out his hand. "I'm Zak and this," he gestured to those surrounding them, "is my family."

Vixin eyed his hand but didn't take it. "And?"

He cracked a teasing smile. "I'm trying to welcome you into the fold."

It was her turn to laugh. "I'm not here to join your little fan club."

He furrowed his brow. "Then why did you follow us?"

She shrugged. "Seemed the best thing to do at the time, but I'll be going now."

"You're new to this world, aren't you?" Vixin ignored him and didn't slow her steps. "Don't you want answers about the magic?"

At that, she paused and glanced over her shoulder. "There's no such thing as magic."

"There is here." Zak held out one hand and particles crystalized from thin air, forming a semi-solid sphere in his hand. The water inside moved in lazy circles, reflecting the firelight. After a moment, the particles broke apart and fell to the earth like rain.

Vixin's lips parted and her gaze traveled from one face to the next in search of anyone who'd be just as surprised as she was. None were.

"Come on, dinner will be ready soon." He turned without waiting for a response to address Anton and Blitz. "I assume you're with her?" They nodded. "Then you're welcome too." Zak helped the two boys to their feet. The rest of his crowd seemed to ignore her after that, settling themselves into a routine they'd probably done dozens of times.

Vixin stood rooted to the same spot, trying to piece together what she'd seen. It could have been a cheap trick. A ploy to add to his numbers. But...the vines. That certainly wasn't a trick. She could still see the man's blood seeping from his mouth. Through his clothes. She'd…she'd killed him.

Vixin took a breath and finally seated herself against a tree, watching those in Zak's company walk back and forth. Some manned the fires, others skinned animals, and the remaining few took stock of their new collection. She shifted her attention back to the trees. They shouldn't linger. This camp wasn't that far away from the place they'd just robbed. It would take nothing for—

"Don't worry about them." Zak tried handing her a chunk of cooked rabbit, the creature impaled on a stick, but she turned away. "Go on, take it."

"I don't need your charity."

"It's not charity. We all work to help one another. Everyone has a job to do."

"You don't know me or whether I'll stay."

He shrugged. "Doesn't matter. You were there. You played a part."

Her stomach growled and she eyed the rabbit.

He chuckled, "Take it."

Vixin took the rabbit and tore through its center without another thought. She chewed in silence, Zak's eyes heavy on her as he bit into his own.

"I know you're curious, but probably not going to ask." Particles formed around them and Vixin stiffened. He held up his wrist and a dark blue stone reflected the firelight. "I can control the element of water." He pointed to her wrist. "And you can control earth."

Vixin finished chewing and eyed her bracelet. "That's what the vines were?"

Zak nodded. "Some people get the hang of it quicker than others, but anyone with a colorful stone has the ability to control an element."

"How do you know this?"

He shrugged. "Figured it out." Yeah, like she was going to believe that. "We're surrounded by plants out here, why not try it?"

She tore another piece from the rabbit and stared at the ground. Shadows from the fire flickered around them, but his particles never left the air. She poked one and a water droplet slid down her finger. Vixin eyed it curiously and placed her hand on the ground, running her fingers through the dirt. Could something like magic really exist?

She focused as she'd done so many times. Skills often required concentration, and if magic were real—she jumped when something moved beneath the earth at her command. It was like an extension that pulsed beneath her fingertips. Dozens, no hundreds, of tiny lights just waiting to be lit. Seeds, roots, all manner of things wriggling, waiting. Like they were a part of her but weren't.

Vixin centered her attention on one directly beneath her hand. She pulsed what she could only assume was energy into the tiny particle. It shifted. Grew. Until something rustled beneath her palm. Vixin raised her hand and the seedling unfurled its leaves, rising to where her hand hovered just above it.

Her mouth gaped as she continued to feed it, watching it grow larger and larger, like a time-lapse video right before her eyes.

"Wow."

Zak's voice startled her, and her gaze shot toward him. He stared at her small creation as if he'd never seen magic himself.

"You just—I've never seen someone try and just, do it." He shifted his attention back to her. "So, what's your story?"

In response Vixin ripped another bite from her rabbit, pointedly ignoring his question.

He laughed, more to himself than at her. "All right then, maybe later. In the meantime, make yourself comfortable. We leave in the morning."

"Where to?"

He glanced back. "Stick around and you'll see."

She huffed. After they'd settled for the night, Vixin seriously considered leaving. Anton and Blitz would be fine now, but something kept her glued to the spot against the tree. Zak had set up lookouts, to her approval, to ensure no one snuck up on them.

She'd stick around long enough to see what their morning travels promised and then decide if she'd be better off on her own.

3

THE GIRL AND A HEIST

Vixin woke before sunrise, watching those who stirred around her and taking special note of the lazy and carefree. Only a few seemed to resent their current situation.

To her dismay, resentment or not, they all answered to Zak, rushing toward him with questions and successes alike. Vixin still wasn't sure what to think of him.

The particles he'd formed in the air last night had to be an illusion. They *had* to be, but—she spread her fingertips over the ground. Sure enough, those same lights responded. She didn't bother feeding any of them. Knowing they remained was enough to confirm her new reality.

Magic. She never imagined such a thing could exist. It defied science. Logic. But the question of why still remained. Why here? Why now?

"They're back!" Vixin's head shot in the voice's direction. She stood, ready to draw her daggers or run, but when the small group embraced those at the edge of camp, she relaxed her hold and headed toward them.

Anton and Blitz gave her a passing glance as she zigzagged through the people. Perhaps this small group had been part of what Zak spoke of last night. Maybe they'd been sent for answers.

Zak all but sprinted to the stocky boy in their center, wrapping his arms around his neck like some long-lost lover. For all she knew, they could be.

"They're in the fourth realm already, just like I said they'd be. We'll be out of this hellish game and back home in no time!"

Zak glanced at her, cleared his throat and tilted his head in her direction. The new arrival took note of her and chewed his lip. He tried and failed to lower his voice as she stalked closer. "She doesn't know?"

"Know what?" Irritation seeped into her voice.

"She just got here last night," Zak said, ignoring her question.

"Oh." The stranger rubbed the back of his neck. "My bad."

Zak sighed. "She was going to find out eventually."

"Find out what?" she growled.

"Maybe you should sit down."

"I'm fine where I am."

Zak held out his hands. "Relax, I was going to tell you, I just didn't want you to freak out is all."

"If you don't—"

"We're in a game."

"A what?"

"A game, you know, like the ones you play on your phone. Chronopoint?" Vixin's mouth opened a fraction. "Don't ask me the details because I can't explain it, but we've all been put inside a game and essentially we have to beat it to get out."

Her mouth opened again and closed as her gaze roamed between Zak and the newcomer. She waited for their laughter, a snicker that would tell her they were joking, and it was just some stupid initiation rite for the new members. But both continued staring.

"That's the most outrageous thing I've ever heard."

"But it explains the magic, right?"

She didn't answer, so Zak turned back to his companion, keeping a wary eye on her. "We're ready to head to the second. The portal is right around the corner and—"

Vixin spun on her heel and stormed off. How utterly ridiculous. Who did they think she was? Some kind of fool? A game, how moronic—

"Vixin!"

She didn't stop at Zak's voice. Instead, she marched straight through the people and then the trees, determined to put as much space between herself and their insanity as possible. Let them all die out here believing what they wanted.

"Vixin, wait up. Hey." Zak grabbed her elbow and her fury split the ground. Greenery of all sorts sprung up in mass numbers, wrapping around his body in a deadly vise that secured his limbs and lifted him from the ground.

She stared at his wide-eyed horror for a moment, willing herself to calm so she could speak. "Stop following me."

"Would you just wait a minute and listen? This is why I didn't tell you right off. Everyone thinks it's crazy. Look at what's around me right now, does this look like anything that could happen in the real world?"

Vixin paused, her blood racing as she tried to digest the concept of magic. *Magic.* It didn't exist, just as she'd said, but…her gaze lingered on the greenery surrounding him, holding him captive at her will.

"Look, it's all right to be scared—"

"I'm not scared." And she wasn't. At least that's not what it felt like. Confused yes. Unsure about the whole situation? Absolutely. But scared? She knew how to take care of herself.

"Fine, then you're not scared, but don't go running off by yourself."

"Why?"

"Because there are other things out there. Monsters, creatures like you've never seen." She was silent. "Please, just come back with me, stick around for a while and once you know what you're up against, if you want to leave, I won't stop you."

She eyed him, debating. Was it worth it to stick with a group? She could care for herself, yes, but she needed to think rationally. They knew things she didn't. Or thought they knew things. What were the chances they were right? Could the answer be something so outlandish?

Vixin huffed and relented. "Fine, but you're going to tell me everything, no matter what you believe I can or can't handle."

Zak nodded. "That sounds fair enough." She eyed him, then stalked back toward the camp. Zak called after her. "Aren't you going to help me out of this thing?"

VIXIN STARED at the swirling mist they called a portal. Zak claimed it'd take them to another realm. A place similar to where they stood now, yet different enough to warrant travel. She clenched her teeth, certain a single step inside that inky blackness would be her one-way ticket to hell.

She stared at the swirling mist and then into the void itself. It was alive, she was sure of it. It wriggled and moved, pulsing as if a creature were breathing. Or hands were waiting to clutch around her throat and devour her whole.

The air that poured from the portal chilled her to the bone and Vixin desperately fought against the urge to flee as fast as her feet could carry her. No life surrounded the purple tendrils floating like morning fog. It was cold. Desolate. As if it sucked life straight from the source.

Zak's people filed through one by one. Some hesitant, others uncaring. Zak stayed behind, encouraging those who were reluctant.

Vixin swallowed hard. She'd told Zak she wasn't afraid, and she hadn't been. But that was before now.

Another person entered the icy void of death and their body stretched beyond human limits before getting swallowed by the darkness. Vixin's heart pounded as she took another step forward, the last in a single line.

She stopped when she and Zak were the only two left. "Are you sure this is safe?"

Zak held out his hand. "I've been through it before. There's nothing to worry about." He flashed her a grin, but it did nothing to ease her nerves.

She eyed his outstretched hand, took a breath, and marched right past him. Vixin didn't stop and her pride prevented her from simply sprinting through like the scared little girl she was.

Icy fingers crawled over her skin as Vixin stepped into the blackness and closed her eyes. She took several shallow breaths and her mind spun as she imagined her body stretched and twisted in a way that should have killed her. She simply kept her legs moving, walking without a solid foothold.

Nausea crawled through her stomach and she clenched her teeth. Her hands tingled, but before panic could set in, Vixin's feet hit solid ground. She stumbled but remained upright and opened her eyes to find Zak's companions to her front. Zak emerged a second later.

The large pathway before them caught her attention first. It was straight. Completely straight. As if someone had used an eraser to simply delete part of the landscape. Not a single bush or tree sprouted. Only dirt and patches of grass. Maybe Zak and his theories weren't so crazy after all.

Zak raised his voice for everyone to hear. "We'll move until nightfall. Sam has a new location for us to hit. You all know the drill."

And just like that, they obeyed. Sam was the new arrival from yesterday who'd slipped up about being confined in a gaming world. A world supposedly made from virtual influences yet felt as real as the one back home.

Her mind spun just thinking about it. Ten realms total, each different from the last. Those stationed at the front lines currently resided in the fourth realm, waiting for their scouts to find passage to the fifth.

Vixin's stomach gave a violent toss and she clamped a hand over her mouth. Her gaze darted between people. Zak was an ever-growing thorn in her side and would likely chase—she darted from the group, sprinting from the clearing before retching behind the nearest tree.

The contents of her breakfast splattered on the ground, but despite its empty state, her stomach heaved again and again. Tears pricked the corners of her eyes and it took Vixin several moments to settle herself. So much for a hot meal.

She groaned at the crunching footsteps behind her. Vixin took a few more steadying breaths, wiped her mouth, and leaned against the opposite side of the tree before looking at him.

"It happens to most of us," Zak said.

"Every time?"

"Just the first time through." He looked her up and down as if gaging whether she'd be able to go on. She almost snorted. "Ready to go?"

Vixin pushed off the tree and followed. Thankfully, Zak didn't mention her episode to anyone and he fell back into his leadership role. As they traveled, he passed food to those who needed it and unrolled blankets for those chilled by the early spring air. He went far to ensure their comfort despite the impossible circumstances.

Vixin furrowed her brow. What made him care so much? She'd never have been that way if people followed her. In fact, she hadn't babied Anton or Blitz at all. Her philosophy was learn or die. Survival of the fittest.

Dusk fell and Zak veered them from the trail to an area that appeared as though it'd been used before. It was far enough away from the main path that no one would notice them. As long as they didn't light a fire.

Vixin sighed at the first sign of a spark.

She eyed each member in the group, but her gaze ultimately fell on Zak. He tightened a sword at his side and shoved a knife in his boot. He caught her gaze and a glimmer of a smile appeared on his face before he approached.

"Want to come with?"

"Where to?"

"To scout the perimeter of our next target. See what we're up against."

"Why ask me?" He had plenty of capable people.

Zak shrugged. "Why not you? Besides, that little gift of yours could come in handy."

Vixin crossed her arms. "So you're using me."

Zak let out an exasperated sigh. "Would you stop over analyzing everything? I just thought you might enjoy it." When she didn't respond, he disappeared through the trees. She took several moments to consider the negatives, then ultimately decided sitting here with these fools would bore her to tears.

Vixin followed the sound of his footsteps through the forest and caught up to him easily. "Don't you feel guilty?"

Zak glanced back at her, the setting sun illuminating his face. "Not really, we don't steal from those that need it."

"You realize that doesn't make sense."

"I mean we don't steal from people who would suffer because of it. That's why we scout. Most places are supported by larger groups."

At least he paid attention to details. Some details at least. "Do you keep everything for yourselves?"

He shook his head. "We trade some of it but keep most of the food. There are people who still need weapons and clothes from the first realm so we try to supply them with any extras we can grab."

"Aren't you the charitable soul?"

He flashed her a toothy grin. "Not in the slightest. Like I said, we trade most things."

Vixin scoffed, but Zak seemed to ignore it.

If they did trade items for other supplies, then where were they? What had they gained from traveling back to the first realm?

Zak shifted to a trot and Vixin did the same. He often stopped to offer his hand when they came to a felled tree, but time and time again, Vixin swatted him away. The less contact, the better.

"What made you resort to stealing?" she finally asked.

"You sound as if you disapprove."

"There are other ways to go about it."

He raised a brow. "You didn't seem opposed to it a few days ago."

Vixin glared at him. She had been stealing, but—

"I needed supplies. It was a onetime thing."

"We need supplies too."

"Well, you weren't just attacked by a group of boys trying to cut your head off."

Zak stumbled. "What?"

"Forget about it. I handled them."

He gaped at her and cleared his throat before resuming their walk. "The reality is that no one is caring for those left in the first realm. Most who have progressed raided the supplies. Since they're able to care for themselves now, I think it's only fair to return the starting materials, if you will, back to their rightful place."

"Sounds like you don't care for the larger groups."

He shook his head. "It's not that. They're just—they have a goal in mind. So they tend to forget the people left behind."

"You don't plan on joining them?"

"Hell no. I'm not risking my life for anyone that's not family."

"You've called them that twice now."

"Because that's what they are. We take care of each other, watch one another's backs. What else would you call them?"

"Is that what you're trying to make me? A member of your family?"

"If you'll let me."

"Why?"

He shrugged. "Do I need a reason? Maybe there's just something about you I like."

Vixin flushed and turned away. She kept quiet after that, following Zak through the growing dark until light drew her attention ahead. Both slowed and quieted their footsteps as they inched toward the town. At least Zak was quieter than Anton.

The light came from two braziers sitting on either side of the front gate. She eyed the guards.

Zak inched closer, knelt at her side, and whispered, "Looks like two guards by the gate and another in the tower."

Her eyes roamed over the rickety tree house he was calling a tower. It looked like it'd been built by a three-year-old. Vixin pointed. "Three towers."

Zak squinted in the dark. "They'll have long-range weapons, so we'll need to take them out first."

A twinge of panic shot through her body. "Guns?"

Zak chuckled. "No. Bows. But they aren't any less dangerous."

"Damn. We really have been thrown back in time."

"Something like that." Zak jerked his thumb back toward the trees. "Let's get the others and make a plan."

VIXIN KNELT outside the wall's edge, glancing through a crack between the planks. She eyed the guards, counting the seconds between their back-and-forth movement. One. Two. Three. Vixin wrapped her vines around herself, Zak, Sam, and a handful of others. They rose over the wall and scattered upon hitting the ground on the other side. Each had their orders.

She took a breath and pressed her body against a nearby wall as another guard made his rounds. Three towers and she was to take out one. She wasn't worried about her role of course, it'd be easy, but if the others messed this up—Vixin shook her head. She couldn't think about them. If she let herself get distracted, then she'd be the one to mess up their plan.

Vixin headed for the ladder, pausing to check its stability. A rough storm would blow it down for sure, but it seemed sturdy enough for now. She hoped. She eyed the guards. Bord. Tired. A smile crawled to her lips. A perfect target.

Vixin eased herself onto the steps, tugging at the greenery to follow.

It twisted along the rails like a shadow, an extension of herself.

Zak had seemed uneasy about her untested abilities, but she'd waved off his concerns. It wasn't like she had to rely upon the magic to fulfill her part of their plan. It was simply a convenience. And a perfect opportunity to test her limits.

Vixin peeked her head over the uppermost floor to find a guard with his back turned. She hoisted herself up on silent feet and slammed the hilt of her dagger in the back of his head. Vixin secured him with the plants and ran back down the stairs.

One down. Hopefully she wouldn't have to assist with the others. Even though their planning was sound, Vixin couldn't be sure how many successful heists they'd actually pulled off.

She crouched at the rendezvous point, the first to arrive. Minutes ticked by and Vixin kept her breathing calm. If the others were caught, an alarm would sound, and she'd be long gone before anyone could even think about catching her. She knew how to get in and out safely. If they didn't, that was on them.

Footsteps skidded through the dirt and Sam appeared with a very winded Zak following.

Zak grabbed his knees. "You purposely gave me the big one," he accused Sam.

Sam winked, then gestured the two toward the storehouse. No one guarded it. She waited. Watched. But no guards were patrolling the area.

"Do we just walk in?" Sam asked.

Zak glanced around and spoke before she could. "They've been warned." She followed his gaze as it traveled from house front to house front. No one stood in the street. "There," he pointed. "See the tracks? They moved something heavy. Today from the looks of them."

Vixin smiled. Well, at least he was good for something. She furrowed her brow as a thought came to mind. "How many times have you hit these people?"

"None, but we aren't the only ones out there and unfortunately there are others who take a more violent approach."

Sam shifted on his feet. "Should we abort?"

Zak shook his head. "We still have the distraction."

"That's meant for emergencies."

"It'll be fine." Zak turned to her. "You might want to cover your ears."

He nodded to Sam who gave a reluctant sigh before scampering off. Zak placed both hands over his ears and hunkered down. Vixin simply stared at the empty street, wondering what kind of traps they might have laid. Physical? Magical? Her gaze drifted to the rooftops, but there weren't any shifting shadows to cause alarm.

She had just started tugging at her magic when a resounding boom echoed across the area and rattled her core. Vixin's hands shot to her ears, sure her drums had ruptured from the vibrations alone. Another boom cracked the silence and Zak tugged on her arm as people shot from house after house, weapons drawn.

He pushed her forward and Vixin all but growled at him. She didn't need to be told to move, but Zak ignored her and peeked around the opposite corner. Her ears rang with the aftershock and another boom echoed that had Vixin clenching her teeth so hard she was sure they'd break. Great, as if she needed hearing loss during a time like this.

Zak's comrades leapt from their hiding places and Vixin followed Zak toward the storehouse. She should run. Everyone had been alerted and her hearing was definitely off, but when no one opposed them, Vixin couldn't bring herself to abandon the goal.

Zak lifted the wooden bar from the doors and kicked them open. Boxes, weapons, and clothes were scattered inside, stacked messily as if someone had been in a hurry to move them.

Each individual grabbed something and headed out. She pocketed a few things and picked out a handful of weapons before shouldering a pack. Within seconds they were darting back toward the trees.

Someone on her left shouted and Vixin twisted around in time to see the young man engulfed in flames. His screams echoed down to her core, but before she could react, water drenched the surrounding area. Zak skidded to a halt at his side and dropped his load to wrap an arm around his companion.

In another flash of blinding light, fire shot from the shadows again and spun toward her like a missile. Vixin rolled to the right, her heart hammering as she scanned the area for their attacker. More flames lit up the night, spiraling around a body stalking toward them. Magic or no, how was she supposed to fight against fire?

"Let's go," Zak yelled.

Vixin shifted on her heel, but the fire user attacked, sending several spears of light their way. She couldn't dodge them all but could her magic—water collided with the flames in midair, and steam rose from the opposing forces. He attacked again and Zak dropped his companion to defend.

The two elements fought, a wave pushing against living flame. Zak gritted his teeth in concentration then fell to one knee. Chaos ensued around them and Zak wasn't the only one in a heated conflict. They needed to get out of here. Now.

Vixin shoved her magic into the earth and pulled at the dormant seeds beneath their feet. She knew what needed to be done.

Plants burst from the earth like a violent monster. The leaves unfurled and thorns raced for their assailant. It spiraled, then slammed into him, carving a deadly path through his flesh. The man screamed, wrapping himself in fire as he tried to fight off her vines. She could almost feel the blood rolling down the stems. Vixin took one step toward him, but Zak's call had her whipping back around.

"Let's go!"

Reluctantly, Vixin turned from the still screaming man. He was fading and she wished she could take the time to make the rest of his companions do the same.

Vixin bounded through the trees after Zak and took his pack so he could focus on carrying his injured companion. Burns ran up and down the young man's arms and she cringed at the thought of the pain.

Once again, the enemy didn't pursue them and Vixin wondered why. If someone were to attack her camp, she'd give chase until every last one of them paid.

When his breathing turned haggard, Zak set his companion on the ground, the young man hissing through his teeth. Vixin glanced at the bubbles forming along his arms and turned away. He needed a hospital, but if Zak's theory was true, then hospitals didn't exist in this world.

Sam emerged from the trees a moment later and his eyes locked on Zak then shifted to the boy on the ground. Family. Is that why they had such anguished looks on their faces? Sure, she felt for the boy, but the pain Zak and Sam felt seemed...different. Deeper.

Sam placed both hands over one arm and a faint glow emitted from his palms. Vixin stilled and everything went silent. She couldn't tear her gaze away this time as the bubbles receded. The skin patched itself together, the redness giving way to new skin as if he were being burned in reverse.

Vixin's mouth gaped as she watched Sam shift to his other arm, focusing on the worst parts first. She almost couldn't believe it. Zak had mentioned the elements, but she never imagined the ability to heal. Had Zak not wanted to freak her out again, as he'd so eloquently put it, or had it simply slipped his mind? How far did healing go? Could it repair internal wounds? Bring someone back from the brink of death?

Once healed, Zak placed a pack under his friend's head and stood. He instructed the others to head back to their camp. Only Sam stayed behind.

Vixin still couldn't tear her gaze away from the young man lying on the ground. He would have died. There was no doubt now. Not from the wounds themselves, but from the aftermath of them. After watching his skin knit itself back together, she could envision the weeks of changed bandages and the smell of rotting flesh. But now—

"What the hell was that?"

Vixin raised a brow at Zak's tone and glanced behind her, sure he was addressing someone else. "Excuse me?"

"You could have killed that guy."

"What guy?"

Zak gave a frustrated snarl. "The one back at the camp."

"You mean the one trying to kill us?"

He gave her a blank stare. "You don't know—"

"Oh, I think I do." She gave his friend lying on the ground a pointed stare.

Zak worked his jaw. "We don't kill people Vixin."

She crossed her arms. "Maybe you don't, but if someone comes after me with the intent, I'm not holding back."

Silence passed between them and Zak took a settling breath. "Look, I know we're in here because of a game, but that doesn't mean it is one. If we die in here, that's it. Game over."

"And that's supposed to what? Make me feel guilty?"

"Yes. No. I don't know all right?"

She glared at him. "Reality check. Without me, you and your friend would have died today, so how about a little more gratitude and a little less of your moral bullshit."

Zak opened his mouth to respond, but instead clenched his fists and let out a defeated sigh. "Come on, let's get back to the others."

Zak and Sam draped the arms of their friend over their shoulders and carried him through the trees. She followed on near silent steps, keeping her ears and eyes peeled for anything out of place.

Vixin let her magic fan out, grazing the plant life in all directions. They reached out to her in return, letting her pulse energy through their branches, feeling for anything unusual, before slipping away again. Animals lurked in the treetops, but nothing that would deem them easy prey. Even with an injured member of their party.

She knew how to identify plants by sight, but now she had a new method. Their energy. Each had a different signature attached, almost like people had fingerprints. The vines were the easiest to identify. They carried a strong light, only dimmed by the surrounding trees. Flowers were more delicate, and the poisonous ones carried a bite that reminded her of spicy food. She half wondered if she'd be immune to their effects.

Upon reaching camp, Zak took the full weight of their companion who was still dragging his feet. She supposed healed or not, he needed rest. So did she, but Sam turned to her when Zak was out of earshot.

"If he won't say it, I will. Thank you."

Vixin clenched her jaw. "He's delusional if he thinks he can do what you guys have been doing and escape without hurting anyone."

"I know." Sam walked after him, leaving her to wander toward her normal spot. A place on the outskirts against a tree. At least here no one bothered her. Usually.

A short while later, Vixin took note of Zak wandering around the center of their camp. He stared at the fires, at the people, and finally toward her. It seemed she wouldn't get to sleep just yet.

Zak took his time coming over and stopped several paces away. He shuffled his feet and she resisted the urge to scream at him while he fought some internal battle with himself. If he wanted to say something, he should just say it.

"Can I sit?"

Vixin gestured toward the ground. "Not like I can stop you."

Zak wrung his hands together, then sat and folded his legs. Neither spoke for a time.

"I'm sorry I yelled at you. I just—would it really be so easy for you to..."

"To kill someone?" she finished. Zak nodded and Vixin let out a long sigh. "If I had to think about it? I don't know, but in the moment, if it's me or them, I'll do what I have to, to survive."

"And if they have a family?"

She shrugged. "That kind of thinking will get you killed." Zak went silent again. "I've never killed anyone, if that's what you're worried about. Sure, I grew up hunting and doing crazy stuff, but I'm not heartless."

A small smile tugged at the corner of his mouth. "That's not what I was thinking at all."

"Then what?"

"I'm just hoping you don't disappear in the middle of the night."

Disappear? "Why would I—" Realization dawned on her and Vixin had to resist the giggle that tried to escape. "I'm not that easily scared off and you guys have become a little too convenient for me to just up and go. Besides, I like the cooking."

Zak chuckled. "I'll be sure to give Sam your regards." He looked at her for another long moment and stood. "Goodnight Vixin and thank you."

She didn't reply and as Zak walked back toward the center of camp, Vixin curled in on herself and let her thoughts drift. Killing. She'd done it once already and she still wasn't sure if it bothered her or not.

4

THE GIRL AND A FRIEND

They trudged through the forest like a herd of elephants. Every single one of them. If people or the *things* Zak had mentioned found them, it'd be no one's fault but their own.

Vixin marched along the outskirts, scanning the trees, the ground, and everything else the fools around her failed to notice.

They'd entered the third realm three days ago and had already hit two more camps along the way. Thankfully, those two had been less prepared than their previous target and Zak's group escaped without so much as a scratch.

Days ago, those around her were barely carrying any supplies. Now, many had packs slung across their shoulders and new weapons in their belts.

She idly wondered how much they'd gather before heading back to the first realm, or wherever Zak claimed to share his treasures. Maybe he'd been lying before. Perhaps he kept it all for himself, tucked away in a thieves' den somewhere.

She eyed his back. But that would require him being a good liar. And she doubted that very much. Not based on his character, of course, but there were signs when someone lied. A tilt of the eyes, a shift in body language. He'd have to be a master of himself to lie to her. Though half-truths didn't seem beyond him.

He'd eased back toward the middle of their group already, walking at a slow pace while talking to yet another of his followers. He did that every day. Started out by leading the line and then slowing down to speak to almost everyone as the day wore on. Vixin had counted forty-seven in total.

He glanced over his shoulder, eyes scanning until they finally landed on her. They always landed on her, like he was keeping track of her whereabouts, afraid she might disappear.

He talked and talked and talked. Smiling and laughing with the others. But when it came time to talk to her? Silence. She should enjoy that, really, but it irked her. Why could he be so merry with the others and then with her—nothing?

Zak glanced her way again and offered a grimaced smile when she met his gaze. A rush of annoyance flew through her and Vixin clenched her fists.

He hadn't stopped by her spot on the outskirts of camp. He hadn't invited her on their heists, though it didn't stop her from going. And now, he wouldn't even speak to her, yet somehow felt gawking was acceptable.

She'd had enough.

Vixin stalked toward him. She'd get to the bottom of this right now. Whether it was from her seemingly unpleasant company or the fire user's almost death, Zak was going to tell her exactly what was on his mind.

Vixin grabbed his elbow while he was in mid-conversation and spun him around. "What's your problem?"

Many turned to stare, but she didn't bother looking their way. Zak just gave her a blank expression, blinking several times as if he didn't understand. He nodded for the others to continue, but their backward glances told her enough about their inner thoughts.

"I'm not sure what you mean?"

Vixin waited for the nosey ones to be out of earshot and even glared at a few who lingered too close. "You keep looking at me."

He cocked his head. "Is that a crime?"

"It is when you don't speak to that person." The way he looked at her now…maybe he did want her gone. Vixin huffed. "If you want me to leave, then just say so."

"What?" His eyes widened. "No, why would I want that?"

"Then what is it? If you have a problem with me, man up and—"

"Can't a guy just admire a pretty girl?"

Vixin went still. The world shifted and everything she thought she'd been piecing together crumbled. She opened her mouth to speak, then clenched her jaw as an unfamiliar warmth filled her cheeks. Zak gave her a sheepish smile and her stomach flipped in response.

"Come on." He held out his hand. Something he hadn't done in days. "We still have a ways to go before we make camp."

Vixin stared at his palm, then his smile, and finally stomped past him, still unable to form words. Zak chuckled behind her and her face heated again.

She picked up her pace, weaving in and out of the people as she made her way to the front. Away from Zak. She was running; she knew, but—*pretty?*

Had she ever used that word to describe herself? Had she ever had a reason to? Vixin suddenly became aware of how she must look. Hair in disarray, dirt caked over her face and clothes. And her *clothes*. Plain and tattered.

Functional, she reminded herself. They were functional and nothing else mattered. She had to survive, not worry about how she looked to others. Especially to some boy who thought he could lead his band of misfits to some kind of glory. She let out a breath. But that wasn't Zak, he didn't seek—Vixin shook her head. Enough.

She slowed her steps, took a breath, and shifted her attention back to the trees. Back to what she knew. Or tried to.

She'd never showed much interest in the opposite sex. Or the same sex for that matter and her father had never brought it up. She smirked at the thought. Perhaps her dad had been thankful for it. She could only imagine his attempt at *the talk* and how awkward that'd turn out to be.

At sixteen, she hadn't given much thought to her future or who might be in it, but that was just it. She was only sixteen and didn't have to. What was a relationship for anyway other than procreating? Her stomach tightened. She'd never be ready for that.

Pretty. Her face heated again and Vixin sighed. She'd always made fun of those stupid, sappy love stories and the garbage they contained. Yet here she was, her heart fluttering at the simple thought of Zak's smile.

He came up beside her like a wraith and she stiffened, suddenly aware of every movement. Her mouth went dry and Vixin swallowed, trying to calm her racing heart. She almost laughed to herself. She'd faced the wilds, animals and people alike. She'd learned to defend herself in the most hands-on way possible and yet here she was, a complete wreck because a boy had called her pretty.

"Something funny?" Zak asked.

Vixin shook her head and decided a switch in conversation was the best route. "You seem to know your way around the realms."

"Like I said, we've been back and forth a few times. The first three, at least. I've seen the portal to the fourth realm, but we haven't gone in yet."

"Why not?"

Zak shrugged. "Why risk messing up a good thing? I know this area and the people in it. It's an easy living."

Vixin smirked. "Easy your thing?"

He cocked his head toward her. "Implying something?"

There went her heart again. That smile. "Sounds to me like you're scared. Don't you think the loot would be better?"

He scoffed. "Yes, but it comes with a higher risk."

"And more fun."

Zak paused and folded his arms. "I'm starting to think you're crazy."

"Have I implied otherwise?"

He shook his head and continued their slow walk. "Fine. I'll take you to one of the better guarded locations and let you see it for yourself."

"I thought you'd never been there?"

"Not in the fourth realm, but there are places in the third we don't hit either."

Zak left her after that to consult with Sam about their camping arrangements. She didn't follow. Instead, Vixin watched from a distance as two magic users struggled to start a fire.

Her gaze drifted to a trickle of water nearby. It rolled off the stones, dripped down a mossy crevice, and finally joined a stream. Vixin pulled her cloak tighter. She'd tried to ignore it, but the dampness had sunk into her bones days ago. If she had to pick a realm to settle in, it wouldn't be this one.

Zak argued with Sam for a long while and though she couldn't hear their conversation, Sam's nervous gestures told her enough. He didn't want them to go. Or rather, didn't want Zak going.

She simply watched, still trying to figure out if Sam was a friend or lover.

Zak shouldered a pack and finally met her at the edge of the ravine they'd climbed into.

"Problems?" she asked.

Zak shook his head. "Nothing to worry about, let's go." Zak grabbed the first exposed root and hoisted himself up. She climbed after, digging her boots into the rocks to ensure she had a proper foothold. Sure, she could have lifted them both up, but she liked the climb, liked the challenge and the feel of dirt beneath her nails.

At the top, Zak turned to offer his hand again, but Vixin shooed him away.

"Is your old man a hard ass or something?"

Vixin clenched her fists, fighting the urge to plant one across his jaw. "And what, exactly, do you mean by that?"

"I just assumed he was the one who, well," he looked her over, "made you the way you are."

Vixin glared at him.

"You're intimidating all right? You seem to have no issue with survival and I'm just asking if your dad had something to do with it."

She cocked her head and a wry smile formed across her lips. "You find me intimidating?"

Zak shook his head and sighed. "Figures that's all you'd hear. No, the others find you intimidating."

She pouted. That explained why he didn't avoid her like the rest. "You should ask Anton and Blitz just how intimidating I can be."

"Why do you think I let you join us in that first raid?" So he *had* been asking about her. "You pride yourself on that, don't you?" He laughed. "They told me the whole thing was pretty wild."

She stepped over a rotted log. "It wasn't anything special. Those boys didn't know what they were doing."

"When did you start learning whatever it is you learned?"

Vixin looked to the sky. "Honestly? Can't remember. Just grew up that way. My mom died at birth, so it's always just been me and dad."

Zak winced. "Sorry to hear it."

She waved him off. "Don't be, I never knew her. But to answer your question, yes, my dad taught me everything. He was in the military but keeps all the details to himself. He just says the world is crazy and that I need to know how to take care of myself."

"Sounds intense."

She shrugged. "It's not like I'm the bunnies and roses type anyway."

"I'll keep that in mind."

Vixin gave him a sideways glance, but Zak fell silent, his eyes scanning the area for once. Vixin's instincts took over and she did the same, crouching down to follow him with near silent steps.

Zak directed her around a pair of crooked trees and crawled toward a moss-covered outcropping ahead. She examined their surroundings, instincts telling her to avoid the too open area ahead, but Zak flattened himself on his stomach and crawled toward the edge.

Vixin followed, feeling the moisture from the rocks seep through her clothes as she inched along. Zak pointed and Vixin followed his finger.

A high wall wrapped around the entire perimeter of a much larger civilization. The towers, nine in all, were a far cry from the pitiful structures she'd seen at their first hit. These were sturdy, ready for the rain and storms and raids. And the guards. All on point, all ready with weapons that looked worn from use.

"They've reinforced themselves."

So they'd been hit too. Just like the first one. Someone else was prowling through their territory. Someone less merciful. Someone willing to take more. What did that mean for Zak's future? Would Zak join them if he weren't given another choice?

Vixin's eyes flashed between the entrances. One at the front, one at the rear, both equally guarded. From up here she could see the extra guards who'd been stationed on the inside of the gate. The extra boards they'd put in place to hold it tight.

A wagon was parked just inside the rear entrance and three men carried boxes from its almost empty interior. They walked toward the center, then veered left, leaving her line of sight for only a moment before popping out again. The door to their warehouse sat open and—every hair on Vixin's body stood on end and her adrenaline spiked. Quicker than her mind could process, Vixin twisted the arm that had reached for her, crushed his face into the dirt, and pushed her blade to his throat.

"Shit, Vixi—"

"Talk."

"What do you mean—" She pressed the blade into his skin and a bead of red rolled down his neck. "Easy," he winced, "I wasn't trying to hurt you."

"Then what were you doing?"

He stammered and she pulled his hair, making him wince again. "Just trying to hold your hand."

Vixin paused, her blood racing through her veins as though she'd just sprinted through the forest. After a moment she released him and backed away, her body still crouched and knife poised.

Zak sat up slowly and rubbed his elbow before wiping the blood from his neck. "Jeez, haven't you ever had a guy flirt with you before?" She blushed but when she didn't respond Zak continued. "You haven't. Have you even been with kids your own age?"

"Of course I have, I've just never gotten close enough to…" Her heart pounded and those weird feelings were stirring again.

"Don't you have any friends?"

The pity in his gaze fueled her temper. "Does it look like I have friends?"

He continued massaging his elbow. "No, I guess not."

For the first time in her life, she regretted. Regretted her reaction, her reflexes. It wasn't her father's fault she didn't socialize. He'd tried time and time again, but all she wanted to do was impress him with her skills. Anything more was just a distraction, including friends.

Vixin slid the knife back into her boot and turned from him. "Sorry." She stood and wiped the dirt from her pants. She could have killed him. Maybe that was why she didn't have friends. If she treated them like this…

"Where are you going?"

She shrugged. "Don't know at this point." Had she ever felt worse than this?

Zak sighed. "You know, I'm not that easily scared off either." She tilted her head toward him. "You don't have to leave just because of a little slip up."

"Little?"

Zak gave her that sideways grin that sent her heart pounding. "How about we start over and try the whole friendship thing first?"

"You and I?"

He shrugged. "Why not?"

Vixin chewed her lip. "I don't know if—"

"Come on, what do you have to lose? Just think of it as another skill to add to your arsenal."

Another skill. Yeah, she could do that. She'd read enough books to know how friendships were supposed to work, she'd just never applied that knowledge. Never wanted to.

Vixin offered him a small smile. "Friends then."

Zak turned toward the barricaded village below. "Maybe you can start by teaching me a thing or two about what you know."

A devious smile crawled to her lips. "I've found experience to be the best teacher."

"I CAN'T believe I let you talk me into this," Zak whispered.

Vixin pressed her back against the nearest house, peering around the corner in search of guards.

"Stop complaining." Vixin noted the tracks in the dirt, then pointed. "That's where they were loading the supplies earlier."

Zak peeked over her shoulder, close enough she could feel his breath on her neck. She bristled, her instincts telling her to step away, but she also noted his careful movements. He wasn't touching her without permission a second time.

"And how, exactly, do you expect us to carry it all out?"

"I don't. You wanted to learn."

"This isn't exactly what I had in mind."

Vixin glanced both ways again, then darted across the expanse and pressed her back against the next house. She paused to listen, waited for a passing guard, then gestured Zak to follow. He didn't hesitate.

"Your footsteps are too heavy. Run on the balls of your feet."

"I'm sorry, not all of us are featherweights."

She rolled her eyes at his tone. "My father isn't either."

"Your father was trained—"

"What do you think we're doing?" She shuffled along the wall and Zak kept close. His eyes darted back and forth, but he was examining all the wrong places. He didn't notice the subtle shift in the guard's routine, or the one who'd been drinking too much and would have to relieve himself at—ah, perfect timing.

The man stumbled from his post, waving to another who only nodded, though she could have sworn he was shaking his head in disapproval. A night guard drinking on the job. She'd have skewered him if she was in control.

Vixin counted the seconds until the drunkard rounded a corner, then darted toward their target. The warehouse. She crawled toward the side with a window, the side the drunk had been posted to watch, and Vixin gave it a quick look through before shoving her knife into the windowsill. The glass popped out easily and she lowered it before letting her plants grow into a woody stalk that would give them a lift. Once inside, her plants disappeared back into the ground.

Vixin pointed toward the door and pressed a finger to her lips.

Zak whispered, "I still don't see how this teaches me anything."

Vixin huffed. "Because you aren't paying attention to what I'm doing."

"I don't know what you're doing if you don't tell me."

"You have to watch people. What side are their weapons on? Are they drinking? Do they favor a leg? The guard who left his post did so because he had half a bottle in his hand."

Zak crossed his arms and a smirk played on his lips. "You'd make a great government spy."

"My father would string me up himself before he'd let me work for the government. He claims they're all corrupt assholes."

"What do you want to do with your life then?"

"Asking me what I want to be when I grow up?"

"Maybe."

Vixin shrugged. "Haven't really thought about it. Dad asks me the same question all the time."

"You can't live with him forever."

"Why not? Who else is going to cook for him?" She shook her head. "He'd eat beans straight from a can if I let him." Vixin shuddered. "Men."

"Hey, I've never been known to eat anything straight from a can."

"Probably because your mom cooks for you."

Zak made to protest, and his face went red. "Yeah, well, she seems to enjoy it." He scratched the back of his head and Vixin smiled at him and the shame now playing on his face. At least he'd appreciate his mother more when he returned home. Not that Zak seemed the type to take his mother for granted.

Vixin refocused her attention to the task at hand. They couldn't sit here all night. Boxes lined the interior and weapons hung along the walls. A lot of weapons. And armor. One would think these people were preparing for a war. Is that what it'd come down to eventually? One faction fighting against another.

Vixin crept toward the leather and carefully picked through it. She tugged on a piece, twisting the material in her hands before setting it down to examine another.

She donned a pair of forearm guards, then eyed some long knives hanging against the back wall. The craftsmanship was exquisite. Far better than what she carried now. Someone here knew what they were doing.

"Find anything worthwhile?" Zak eyed her weapons but made no move to reach for them.

"Yeah." She tossed him a vest. "And this ought to fit you."

"Thanks." He glanced around. "So what now?"

"What kind of weapon do you prefer?"

"A sword."

She clicked her tongue. "How typical." Vixin ignored his 'what did you expect' smile and studied the weapons around the room until she eyed one suitable. She picked it up, tested it, then handed the blade to Zak.

He swung it once. "It's light."

"Speed is your friend in a fight. That other one you carry is too heavy. Just leave it here."

"You sound like some old war veteran."

"I'll try to take that as a compliment. *Friend*."

"Of course it's a complement. How many girls do you think would even have a clue—"

"Shh." Too late. She'd noticed too late.

Vines crawled up their legs, twisting themselves around both her and Zak's limbs. Thorns grew from the stems and leaves unfurled in a pattern she recognized. Nothing deadly, but they pinned her arms before she could reach for her new weapons.

Both were lifted from the floor and five guards entered the room, each eyeing them with disdain. The vines holding them captive brought them forward, as if they were floating across the room.

A burly man with a receding hairline lifted his chin to examine them. He stood with one arm draped over his sword and knees bent. Ready. He wouldn't go down easily.

"Looks like we've caught a couple of thieving rats." He glanced her over and then eyed Zak.

Zak struggled and the vines clamped down on him, thorns digging into his flesh until he winced. She remained perfectly still.

Vixin cocked her head. "I wasn't taking anything you'd miss."

He stared at her for a moment, then a smile broke across his pock-marked face. "And you think that somehow justifies your actions?"

She tried to shrug. "I hadn't planned on getting caught."

He shook his head, still laughing. "Well, now you have been, and I don't think you're going to like the consequences."

Vixin jerked her chin toward his guards. "If they were better at their jobs, I wouldn't have been able to sneak in. Honestly, you should be thanking me. Or better yet, why not offer me a job? I'm sure I could teach your men a thing or two."

He marched right up to her, the vein in his forehead bulging. She'd take a slap to the face for that one, but Zak's voice broke the tension first. "Get away from her!"

The man paused, glanced at Zak, then gave him the most sickening smirk she'd ever seen. "Don't worry, you can have her after she's learned a lesson." He licked his lips and lust-filled eyes ran along her body. "Or two."

Just like that, her playfulness vanished. Despicable. The men behind him no different. She remembered a time when her father had warned her about such men. About how dire circumstances could change a person. How power could alter their core values, turn them into monsters or cowards. It was a rarity that people remained who they claimed to be.

Vixin glanced toward Zak, half wondering what kind of man he'd prove to be, but her lips parted upon seeing the fear on his face. Not fear for himself. No, far from it. His eyes darted from her face to the man with a wicked grin and then back to her. He struggled and, in that moment, she knew.

Zak wasn't a coward. He bled as he fought against the thorns, but the blood rolling down his arms wasn't for himself. He bled for her.

Vixin offered him a reassuring smile, but Zak didn't return it. She shifted her attention back to the man still prattling on about what he was going to do to her. Intricate details about all the ways he might teach her a lesson. She'd all but drowned him out. Any moment now—

His companions hit the ground. Their vile leader spun around, his booming voice commanding them to stand until he grabbed his chest and sank to his knees alongside them. The vines fell from Vixin's body and she rotated her wrists to bring circulation back to her fingers.

"Hurts, doesn't it?" Their leader twisted around, spittle dripping from his mouth, but his face hit the dirt floor before he could utter another word.

The vines holding Zak captive fell at his feet. He stared in silence, looking from her to the motionless bodies sprawled before them.

"I don't understand," Zak whispered.

"Poison. Not the most exciting method to get rid of someone, but definitely effective."

He gave her a blank stare.

"I hit their ankles with it earlier. I know you don't like—"

Zak's arms were around her before she could finish her sentence. Her first instinct was to put him on the ground, but something about the look in his eyes made her hesitate. He crushed her body against his, gripping her as if she might disappear any moment.

His entire body trembled, but Vixin remained still, dumbfounded.

"I'm sorry," his voice cracked. "I didn't know what to do. I froze. All those things he said, I should have—"

"Stop." She pushed him away and pinned him with a stare. At least he wasn't crying. Yet. "Everything's fine."

Pain flashed across his face again. "He could have—"

"He didn't and I wouldn't have allowed him to. I'm not the damsel in distress and I don't need a knight in shining armor. It takes practice to react to stuff like this. Practice I've had. Now that you've faced it once, you'll be more prepared next time. Unless, of course, I get to them first."

Zak gave her a half-hearted smile. "You really are one of a kind."

THE PAIR carefully made their way back to camp and Zak kept eyeing her as if she might break down any second. She didn't berate him for it. He cared and though she couldn't fathom why, at least now she knew he wasn't a selfish coward. If she were going to have anyone as a friend, that was definitely a positive quality.

Still, she wondered if he would expend the same kind of energy in a desperate attempt to save any of the others. A selfish part of her hoped not. Vixin silently shoved that part of her away, mentally kicking it to the side.

She split from him as soon as Zak saw Sam's face. They'd want to talk, and she wasn't in the mood to detail every little thing that'd happened.

Vixin settled into her usual spot outside their camp and tugged at a familiar seed just below the soil's surface. She still marveled at how quickly it responded. Almost as if the plant itself sought to please her with its presence.

Blue flowers unfurled from a thin stock that steadily grew and grew until she ceased feeding it. Vixin stared at the deadly plant. She'd always thought killing would feel...different. She should regret, but all she could summon forth was indifference. Vixin furrowed her brow. Was there something wrong with her?

"That's pretty." She startled at Zak's voice. He knelt and reached for the delicate petals.

"I wouldn't touch it if I were you." He paused and she inclined her head. "That's the reason those men are, well, you know."

"Oh." He sat back on his heels and stayed silent for a time. "Are you all right? After all that I mean?"

Vixin snorted. "I'm fine."

"You really weren't scared?"

"I had the situation under control." Zak stared at the flowers. "Were you scared?"

"Terrified," he admitted. "I didn't—" he cut himself off and huffed. "My mind just went totally blank."

"Don't beat yourself up, most people freeze. It's normal."

He let out a long breath. "Normal or not, that sucked."

"Then don't let it happen again. Dwelling on the past doesn't fix anything. You know your weakness now, so fix it."

"Will you help me? Help us?" Vixin stared at him. "We could really stand to learn some of the things you know. Obviously, we can't learn everything, but at this point I feel like anything would help us survive."

"Yeah. I guess I could do that. As long as they're willing to learn."

Zak saluted her. "I will ensure my students are the best you've ever had."

She laughed. "They'll be the only ones I've ever had."

Zak stood, still staring at the flower. "Hey Vixin."

"Yeah?"

"Thank you."

5

THE GIRL AND THE BOY

With morning Vixin woke to a very peculiar feel in the air. Everyone eyed her, but not with the discomfort they'd shown previously. They watched her every move, right down to how she ate breakfast.

She'd never liked being the center of attention, but if she was going to teach someone, she'd rather have them clinging to her every word than ignoring her. Not that she had to do this, if they proved incapable, she could always walk away. If Zak let her.

"We're ready when you are." He sat beside her with a bowl in his hand.

"I think I'll eat first."

"Right, I was just saying." He took a bite of the stew, which by all standards was pretty good.

"What did you tell them exactly?"

"That you were going to teach us some kickass survival skills."

"They'll be disappointed." He raised a brow. "It's not all about the physical. In fact, that's the least of my concerns."

"They'll learn whatever you teach them."

We'll see.

After breakfast, the group gathered in a circle around Vixin and Zak.

She glanced at Zak and then to the people patiently awaiting her instructions. All eyes were trained on her. Faces she'd started to recognize. There were Anton and Blitz. And then Sam, who'd started smiling at her more after hearing of her daring escape. Maybe that's why the others were so willing to listen.

Vixin took a step forward. Last night, she thought she might be nervous, but it was quite the opposite. She felt elated. Empowered. "All right. First thing is first." The mini conversations quieted. "Awareness. Some of you might think this is a boring step so I'm going to show you up front why it isn't. Grab a partner." Some shuffling occurred and she waited for each team to settle into place. Zak stepped closer and a smile tugged at the corner of her lips. He'd certainly regret volunteering himself before the day ended.

"Now close your eyes. You've been beside this person all morning. Likely a lot longer since you've been traveling together. I want you to think about the answers to the following questions.

"First, are they right or left-handed? This is of paramount importance if you run across an enemy. Maybe you know what your partner is, maybe you don't. If you do, props to you. Now, am *I* right or left-handed? Or am I ambidextrous? If I were your enemy would you know how to fight me?

"Open your eyes and see if you were right about your partner." She gave them a few moments. Giggling occurred and her irritation rose, but Vixin shoved it down. "Now what about me?"

They called out their answers and Vixin tried not to shake her head. "You forgot the middle option. It's not often that a person is ambidextrous, but I am. If you were up against someone like me, ninety percent of you would have just died." The giggling ceased.

"In this world, you need to concern yourself with more than simply what hand someone uses. What about their magic? Do your eyes flicker to their wrist? Do you even think about it? What about the guards? What does their body language tell you? Are they tired? Injured? In need of a break?

"With the line of work you do, these are the things you need to pay attention to and it's as simple and as hard as that. When was the last time you glanced at the treetops?" Several eyes shot up. "Could someone have been lurking over you? Your first lesson is to pay attention and we'll be practicing just that."

Vixin drew her blade and faced Zak. He glanced at her, his brow raised, but when she charged, Zak drew his weapon to block her attack.

He staggered back. "What the hell?"

"Good, now put your sword away." He held onto it until she sheathed hers. Murmuring flew through the crowd. "Now, which arm did I attack with? Which did Zak defend with? What foot did he use to step back? Did he falter or was his stance steady? Discuss these things with your partner because this is what we'll be focusing on today."

With Zak's help, they split into several groups. A few squared off while their comrades observed and evaluated. Not only did they take the exercise seriously, but it seemed as though they were learning more about their own abilities as well. About what their reactions would be and how they could correct their mistakes. Perhaps there was hope for them yet.

"Is that a smile?"

She tilted her head toward Zak's voice. "Does it matter?"

"I don't think I've seen you smile since you've been here."

"It's not exactly been a jolly fun time."

"You've got to make the most of it. If you spend the entire time in survival mode, you'll drive yourself crazy."

"Giving me lessons now?"

He crossed his arms and smirked. "I guess I am."

She huffed and turned back to watch the others. The same young man had fallen three times already and couldn't seem to figure out his mistake. Vixin shook her head and walked forward with Zak on her heels.

NIGHT DESCENDED and Vixin seated herself in her usual spot. A few approached her, albeit cautiously, to ask questions and she happily answered. Most revolved around how they could possibly pay that much attention to so many details. She gave them all the same answer. Practice.

With questions done and dinner eaten, Vixin rested her head against a tree and closed her eyes. Zak sat next to her a few moments later and she resisted the urge to huff. "What?"

"I want to show you something."

She cracked one eye open. "It can't wait till morning?"

He looked toward the sky and the full moon rising. "It wouldn't be as epic in the morning."

"If you try to kiss me, I'll break your arm."

He roared in laughter which had a few heads turning. "Noted, I won't kiss you then." Zak stood and held out a hand. She looked at it but didn't take it before standing.

"Where are we going?"

"You'll see."

Vixin crossed her arms. "You had me teach an entire class on awareness and now you want me to follow you blindly into the woods?"

"What's wrong? Don't trust me?"

She scoffed. "That shouldn't surprise you. I don't trust anyone."

"Ouch, I thought we were friends?"

She opened her mouth and closed it again. "Fine, lead the way."

Vixin followed him through the trees, careful of her footing and laughed when Zak couldn't quite do the same. She watched his staggering form and found it difficult to not ask questions. Instead, she contented herself to watching the treetops for anything sinister that had nothing to do with Zak.

Vixin huffed as their nightly stroll continued. "I would like to get some sleep tonight."

"Just a little further, I promise." It seemed forever before he stopped and held the brush back to let her walk through. A pool of water reflected the dark sky and full moon like a sheet of glass.

"You wanted to show me a pond?"

"Not quite." He lifted a finger and ice formed on the tip. "I haven't seen you have much fun since you've been with us, so I thought it was time you did."

"In the middle of the night?"

"Well, it's not like you'd do this in front of the others."

"What do you think I am, broody?"

"Yes."

She opened her mouth to speak, but Zak walked to the edge of the pond and dipped his fingers into the water. Instantly, frozen flakes began crawling across the surface, shimmering and spreading as they made their way across the entire pond.

She took a few steps forward, watching the display. The ice thickened then frost crawled outward toward the trees, up the trunks and into the leaves. It touched the air, giving it a cold bite and flecks of what appeared to be snow swirled in the breeze.

She let out a breath and it became a visible cloud.

"Have you ever ice skated?"

Vixin shook her head. "Not sure we're going to find a pair here anyway."

Zak smiled, lifted one foot, then ran his hand underneath to form a blade. "No need for them." He held his hand out to her leg. Vixin stood there for several seconds, debating all the reasons he could possibly want to ice skate in the middle of the night. It seemed ridiculous. With his abilities he could easily drown her, leave her for dead, but her instincts weren't screaming against it and Zak was...her friend.

Vixin handed him her foot and he took it carefully, running his fingers along the bottom of her boot. A shiver ran through her body as cold seeped through the material.

"You might need to sit down for the other one."

Vixin plopped onto the bank and another stream of cold went through her foot as Zak finished the second blade with precision. She'd seen him use some of his abilities on their runs but didn't realize he could be so accurate with it. She'd tuck that information away for later.

Zak finished working on his other foot then Vixin stared at the clear, icy surface. "I take it you ice skate back home?"

"It's a hobby. There's a rink down the street and everyone from our neighborhood meets up on the weekends. It's decent exercise and keeps us out of trouble as our parents say."

"Sounds like a close-knit community."

Zak shrugged. "We all grew up together, go to the same school, same church, and most of us play the same sports."

"Which are?"

"Hockey mostly." Of course. Zak shifted to his feet, placed one foot on the ice and glided out without so much as a stumble. It was elegant. Perfection. The exact thing she strived for with every challenge she took on.

Zak turned back toward her and slowed to a stop at the bank. He placed one foot on the frozen grass and offered his hand. "Come on, at least let me help you find your balance."

She pursed her lips, glanced at the slippery surface, then decided accepting his offer would be far less humiliating than planting her face on the ice. She tucked her small hand in his, finding a strength in his palm she hadn't expected as he pulled her to her feet.

As soon as her skates hit the ice, Vixin took off faster than she anticipated, but Zak held firm, slowing her down as they glided across the surface together. His hands wrapped around her elbows, preventing a fall she was sure she'd regret in the morning.

"Take your foot in front of the other like this."

"I *have* skated before."

"Really?"

"What do you think my dad does? Keep me locked away in the mountains?"

"Well…"

"I told you, he *tries* to get me to socialize."

"So you guys are really close then."

"We do everything together." Vixin studied her balance. "I think I got the hang of this now."

Zak released her, though he looked reluctant to do so. She put one foot in front of the other and leaned to one side to turn back toward him. She tottered but caught herself before he could come to her rescue. "See? Piece of cake."

"Fast learner."

"Always have been."

"All right hot shot, let's see who's the fastest."

They raced, gliding across the surface with the cold air hitting her in the face. Her nose froze over, her hands stiffened, but the exhilaration flooding through her made all those small inconveniences worth it. Is this what friendship felt like? Is this what her father wanted her to experience?

When her feet were too frozen to go on, Vixin slid to the edge, breathing hard, and Zak came to join her before plopping on the hard ground. He ran his hands over the surface of his blades, and they melted back to water. Vixin sat beside him and he did the same to hers.

"I guess you *can* have fun."

She scoffed. "You just don't know me."

"Does anyone?"

"Not really," she admitted.

"Is that why you originally played the game?"

Vixin crossed her arms for warmth. "I don't know. Maybe, but once I saw the idiotic conversations I wasn't really interested anymore."

"Yeah, people can be pretty stupid, but that's with anything."

"Why did you join?"

"Remember all those neighbors I told you about? We decided to start playing together." He looked at his hands. "Who knew it would lead to something like this?"

"Then they're here too."

He nodded. "I keep hoping to run across them, but in a world this big, what are the chances?"

"Probably not good."

He chuckled. "Blunt as always."

"I don't see the point in lying. The situation is shitty, so why try to doll it up?"

"To make people feel better."

"So people would prefer a lie?"

"Sometimes a lie is easier."

Vixin disagreed, but instead of arguing she lifted her gaze to the clear sky and stars. With the cold air hitting her back it reminded her of home and the nights she'd spent outdoors around a campfire with her dad. "Thanks for bringing me out here."

A pause then Zak leaned forward to catch her attention. "Were you serious before?"

"About what?"

"About breaking my arm."

Her lips parted at the way he gazed at her and something in his eyes had her heart racing. Those strange feelings stirred, tightening her stomach and though she looked away, Vixin couldn't help the shy smile that crossed her face. "I wouldn't push your luck."

Zak laid back and crossed his arms behind his head. "I'll break through that hard shell of yours eventually."

Vixin found herself hoping he would.

6

THE GIRL AND A MISTAKE

With morning, their training continued and somehow she felt... lighter. Vixin smiled a little more and those around her seemed to welcome the shift in her demeanor. With all her talk about awareness, she really should have noticed how she affected the rest of them.

Vixin observed the people around her, struggling with how she should feel. Honestly, she hadn't cared before, and couldn't decide if she should care now. Did she want them close or cautious? Did she want friends?

Zak stood before her, sword raised. "I feel like you're going to accidentally slit my throat."

She smiled at his nervous shift. "Oh, it wouldn't be an accident if I did."

"That's comforting."

Vixin tilted her head. "I'd have to be pretty heartless to kill my friend."

"Will we ever be more than that?"

Her breath hitched and the night before flashed through her mind, but Vixin shook it off, charged, and flipped him over her shoulder. "Depends. Can you stay on your feet?"

He huffed and rose. "Again."

THREE WEEKS later, Vixin readied them for their first day of offensive training. She'd spent the time creating drills where they'd run through the woods, searching for 'attackers' she'd hidden in the trees. Vixin tested their endurance and strength and gave Zak's group a confidence she hadn't seen in them before.

Much to her dismay, Zak insisted there were a few among them who didn't need to participate, and no amount of convincing could get him to see otherwise. Everyone should at least try. Their age didn't matter. Nor did their gender. After a time, she'd simply ignored them. If their comrades wanted to come to their rescue then so be it, but she wasn't about to risk her life on people who wouldn't learn to protect themselves.

Everyone stood at the ready, their stances practiced and at least up to par. Many were still far from perfect, but she couldn't expect perfection in this short amount of time. They'd learn on the fly or die trying.

"Go."

A series of grunts followed her command and Vixin eyed those tossing their partners over their shoulders. Thankfully, Zak had chosen Sam as his partner today, enabling her to observe and correct.

"Again."

They lined up, and another series of grunts followed.

"You," she pointed to a young man, "your stance isn't wide enough. If you want to be able to toss your opponent, you need to be balanced."

He threw up his hands. "What's the point?" Vixin raised a brow. "We have weapons. Not to mention magic. Why do we need to learn hand to hand?"

"You need to learn yourself before you can learn extensions of yourself."

"I mean no offence." He glanced toward Zak. "Honestly, but we were doing just fine without all this extra work."

Vixin crossed her arms. "How tall are you?"

"Almost six foot."

"And how tall would you estimate me to be?"

"I don't know. Five three I guess?"

"Five one, but close enough. And how much do you weigh?"

"Two hundred, give or take?"

"And me?"

"What?"

"How much do you think I weigh?"

"Um, I don't know."

"I'm one fifteen. Now, you have close to a foot and a hundred pounds on me. Pick up a weapon."

"I don't understand."

"I said pick up a weapon. I didn't ask if you understood." He glanced around at the others and did as he was told. "Now, cross your blade with mine and push." He did so halfheartedly but Vixin growled at him. "I said to *push*."

At that, he shoved and Vixin fell onto her backside. Some in the crowd murmured, but she resisted the urge to grimace and picked herself up. "Now do it again."

"I don't—"

"I said, do it again," she yelled.

This time he came at her full force. She ducked under his weapon, scooted her body close to his, and threw him over her shoulder. It was a technique she'd practiced with her father a thousand times.

He hit the ground hard and all those watching gasped.

"You outsize me and believe it or not there will be people who outsize you. When that happens, brute force will not be enough to bring them down. Awareness, sizing up your opponent, attention to detail, all this ties together so don't forget it. Anyone else have questions?" They remained silent. "Good, then get back to work."

"YOU WERE pretty brutal today." Zak sat beside her.

"I don't like being challenged."

"They'll have questions. Daniel might look like a brute, but he's pretty soft on the inside. Maybe go a little easier on them next time?"

"Easier gets you killed. Speaking of, when are we leaving this place? I thought you guys didn't stay in one spot too long?"

"They needed a break and we had everything we needed to get by. But you're right. It is about time to move. We'll probably hit another spot then head back to the second realm to trade out our weapons."

"We haven't even started working on magic."

Zak gave her a sideways smile. "Are you going to convince me you're an expert in that already?"

"I practice every night. I don't see them doing the same."

"Is everything always this hard core with you?"

"Get used to it. I'm not dying here, and I'll utilize every second of every day to ensure it."

Zak lowered his voice. "What if you spend your whole life preparing and die anyway?"

"Then at least I'll go without regrets."

ZAK DIDN'T let her drill them the following day, but Vixin still went around asking about their magical abilities. Even if she couldn't prepare them before their next hit, she could start preparing a training regime.

Vixin stalked through the camp and thoughts of other groups in the realm plagued her. Clearly, someone was nearby and operated with more lenient rules. They were willing to kill, maim, possibly even torture. What would happen if they encountered this group? Zak didn't seem like the type to yield and she couldn't envision a fight ending in their favor.

Vixin glanced at Zak while he conversated with a young man, readying the people he called 'family' to embark on another adventure. Zak leaned to one side, stretching his back and guilt washed through her. She'd caused that. Here they were, getting ready to hit another target and Zak was still feeling the pain from her throw. If that pain hindered his ability—Zak waved, her cheeks heated, and Vixin stormed off to address another she'd seen with a red stone around his wrist.

Will we ever be more than that?

She'd ignored his words but hadn't forgotten them. They were friends, but...more? She'd already messed up the friendship thing so how could she hope to—Vixin shook her head. She couldn't think about that right now. She needed to focus. They had a mission to plan.

ONE LOOK and Vixin knew this was a bad idea. They didn't have a wall to guard them, but wall or no, these people were ready for an attack.

"You should pick a different location," Vixin said.

Zak eyed her. "I didn't think you were one to get cold feet."

"I'm not, but it doesn't feel right. Look how attentive the guards are. Only one seems to be slacking and I'm willing to bet it's only due to lack of sleep. They have traps set up in the grass and who knows what else."

"We're already here, might as well give it a go."

He stood, but Vixin grabbed his arm. "I'm serious."

Zak stared at her then looked back toward the guards. "We'll switch plans then. You're the most apt with magic and have the keenest eye. If you're that worried, function as the backup instead of the assault. If you see something go wrong, yank us out."

"I already see something wrong."

"You *think* something's wrong, that's different. We've done this dozens of times. It'll be fine."

Vixin tsked but let him go. He informed the others and several glanced at her with worried expressions. She half hoped they'd take her advice, talk some sense into Zak, but they trusted their leader more than her it seemed. Fine, let them get themselves killed over stupid pride.

Vixin eyed the guards again and the hair on her arms stood on end. Magic charged the air, causing her own to hum with it. She clutched the knife in her belt.

This night wasn't going to end well.

VIXIN CURSED. She should have seen it. She *had* seen it but couldn't tell where the attack would come from. And now, the whole lot of them were trapped in the center of town, surrounded and unprepared.

People were going to die, but Zak...Zak was her only focus.

Plants burst from the ground and wrapped around the first sentry. He didn't even have time to scream and his eagerness to watch her friends tortured cost him his life.

Friends. Were they *all* her friends now? Should she care about them like Zak did?

Magic crackled through the air, like static before a storm. She could feel the plants wriggling beneath the earth, all poised to deliver a deadly blow. Vixin gritted her teeth and surged her magic through the ground. She wrapped them around the plants ready to strike, strangling her enemies before they could take root.

Vixin could prevent earth magic, but what about the other elements? Judging from her earlier conversations, Zak's people weren't as apt at disabling another's ability. She should have spent a week on it, put her focus on the physical aspects of training instead—

Vixin skidded to a halt just before a group of guards and yanked herself up the side of a building and onto the roof. She scanned the area and crept forward with the moonlight as her guide and paused just outside a ring of people.

Zak stood before his friends, a grimace marring his face. He had one hand outstretched as if he could protect those behind him and another on the hilt of his sword.

She couldn't see the face of the one who spoke next. "You're not talking your way out of this." He raised one arm. "Kill them."

Vixin's skin prickled and the night exploded. Her magic tightened like a lease on a dog's collar. The earth's surface crumbled, but the deadly vines didn't shoot toward her companions. Fire collided with fire and steam rose as water joined the fray.

Vixin jumped from the rooftop, letting her vines impale those directly below her. She drew her knives, slashing the vital points of any who dared close the distance. There could be no mistakes. There could be no mercy.

Sweat rolled down her face and her breathing was already uneven but Vixin shoved through the exhaustion, pouring more energy into the plant life she was struggling to restrain.

Vixin kept her attention on Zak, hacking through her enemies as she moved toward him. A fire user fell with a thick vine protruding from his chest. Another shooting spikes of ice gurgled and hit the ground, clutching at the greenery crawling from his throat.

"Zak!"

He whirled at the sound of her voice and she waved him toward her. Zak kicked the man he'd been fighting and sprinted from those about to converge upon him.

He wouldn't make it. Not with the man to his right about to swing his sword. Not with the two to the left summoning fire and ice.

Fear exploded though her body and her magic responded, ripping from the ground by the hundreds. Thorns impaled Zak's would-be attackers and lifted them into the air.

Vixin focused and her magic rushed toward her like a tidal wave, crashing into the houses on her right and left.

Her vision blurred and she hit one knee, but Zak was on her in seconds, gripping her arm and lifting her from the ground.

Screams echoed from beyond her walls. Screams from their comrades. She wanted to take him and run but one look and Vixin knew. Zak wasn't leaving them behind.

She took a breath and followed Zak back into the fray.

Something exploded to their right and Vixin ducked but Zak didn't stop. It wasn't until she saw Sam that she understood.

Fear crawled down her spine as she took in the numbers. Most possessed some sort of magic and they were converging upon Sam, rallying their strength while hers was depleting. Failing.

Vixin tugged at the sluggish roots beneath her feet and used all her strength to keep the men from reaching Zak as he plunged his knife into the side of an unsuspecting victim. He grabbed his friend's wrist, and charged back toward her, but an air current ripped the two apart.

Sam skidded across the ground beyond her reach and drew his blade to face an oncoming assailant. Zak collided with the earth at her feet, knocking the wind from his chest.

Vixin's heart sank as she gave Sam one final glance. Fire and ice raced toward her in a cruel, twisted current. She dug deep, and with a desperate scream, Vixin harnessed every last drop of magical energy pulsing beneath her skin. It shot from the ground, layering them in a cocoon of vines and thorns.

Her body screamed in agony, every cell feeling as though it were on fire. Zak gasped and Vixin hit her knees. Sweat poured down her face and every breath felt like razor blades digging through her chest, but she couldn't let up. Not until—Zak placed one hand on the ground and ice spread over the grass and up the circular structure guarding them.

Their enemies hit again, and again, and again. The structure groaned and Zak gritted his teeth.

"The right," her voice cracked, but Vixin shouted again, "Hit the right."

Zak didn't hesitate. He blasted a hole right through her structure, grabbed her wrist, and sprinted from the camp as fast as their legs could carry them.

Two sentinels raised their bows, but water shoved them from the roof before they could fire.

She didn't know how many made it out and her heart hurt for those left behind but when Zak hesitated, she grabbed his shirt and shoved him toward the safety of the trees.

He didn't turn back after that, but the look on his face told her of his longing to. To help his friends still screaming. They'd give away his name, of that she was certain. None of them were cut out for torture and why would they be? They were normal people. People born in a time where survival wasn't necessary. She was lucky to have a parent who taught her such skills, but why? Why was she put in a situation like this? In a place where she *had* to fight? Where innocents died.

Black specs swam across her vision and Vixin cursed. She'd overused her magic, forgotten about self-preservation. Their enemies would pursue them, and she didn't even have the strength to keep running. She needed a place to hide. Somewhere safe. If they caught her…

The trees filtered by, the noise fading as they bolted through the forest. Her eyes scanned the area for anything. A burrow. An animal hole. A ditch. But she couldn't focus.

Someone said something, but their voice was muddled, and she turned to Zak's concerned face. His lips moved again, but somehow she couldn't understand him.

A safe place.

Her gaze swept over the blurring landscape.

A safe place…

Vixin fell right into Zak's arms.

7

THE GIRL AND A HOME

A fire crackled, shifting and twisting its way through the dark, blissful corners of her subconscious. Vixin balked at the noise and light, fighting to escape, but it yanked her right back into a painful waking world.

She groaned and a familiar face blocked out the fire a second later. "Hey." Thankfully his voice was soft, almost a whisper, which either meant they were still in danger or others were sleeping. "Easy does it." Zak assisted her to a seated position.

She'd been exhausted before, pushing her body to its limits just to see how far it could go, but this...this was something different. A new level that made not sleeping for three days feel like a walk in the park.

"Are we safe?" Her voice cracked and Zak handed her a waterskin. She downed half the contents before he responded.

"Relatively. At least for the moment." Comforting. Vixin counted the heads around her. Then counted again. Twelve. Her and Zak made Fourteen. Less than half had made it out.

A strangled sob met her ears and Zak dipped his head. "I'm sorry. If I would have listened to you..."

She didn't comment. Not everyone needed a verbal reprimand after a mistake, sometimes the consequences were enough. Not that she had much room to talk.

"Thank you," Zak continued. "If you hadn't come for us…"

Her heart pounded at the mere thought. "I couldn't just leave you." Cheesy maybe, but the truth.

His lips lifted a little, but she'd hardly call it a smile. Vixin finally let herself look at their faces. Anton and Blitz were missing. As was Sam…

"We should head to the rendezvous point," someone said. "There's still a chance."

"Rendezvous point?"

Zak sighed. "We set up a place, just in case we ever got separated." He glanced at the faces around them, seeming to take in their exhausted state. "We need somewhere to lay low anyway."

A cry of pain escaped Vixin's lips as Zak helped her stand, every joint feeling as though it'd been torn from the socket and relocated. Zak kept one arm around her back to keep her steady and she didn't protest.

They were hungry, tired, pitiful in every sense of the word as they trudged through the woods, taking careful measures to remain hidden. None of them would survive a second aggressive encounter.

Her strength returned with each step and Vixin slowly carried her own weight. Judging from the bags beneath his eyes, Zak was just as exhausted as she felt.

Magic. A curse and a blessing all in one. A weapon she could utilize and yet one that could destroy her if she weren't careful. One mistake and she could pass out within an enemy's territory never to wake again.

Vixin glanced at Zak. Dirt covered his clothes, dark bags hung beneath his eyes, but it was the hollow look on his face that drew her attention the most. She'd been searching for somewhere safe before her blackout and in that moment, nothing had felt safer than Zak's arms. Even now, with one arm still draped over her shoulder she felt...protected.

"Thank you," she said. "For not leaving me either."

"Just repaying the favor." She knew that wasn't true. Even if she'd left him behind, Zak—a twig snapped to their right and Vixin whirled. She went for her blades but found them missing. Zak drew his and stood before her, frost already covering the ground at his feet. Her breath clouded in the suddenly brisk air.

Someone screamed as Anton walked through the trees, followed closely by Blitz. And then Zak was running, embracing the friend she was sure had been lost. Sam. More emerged from the woods, far more than she'd hoped to find.

Sam went to work, assessing each of them, using his magic to heal wounds that could have waited another day. When he got to her, Vixin just smiled and tilted her head toward Zak. They had to be the luckiest people alive.

THEY'D HIDDEN the rendezvous point deep inside a cavern, away from any well-trodden path. Vines had been draped over the entrance and brush had grown so thick Vixin wasn't even sure the animals would find it. To say she was impressed would have been an understatement.

It only took a few minutes for another earth user to clear them a path inside and then cover the hole over as if it'd never been disturbed. A narrow entrance guided them through the first few feet and then opened into a large expanse that provided more than enough room for everyone to fan out.

Vixin leaned against the nearest wall and slid down it to rest her aching feet. She stared at the hole in the top of the cave, just wide enough to give them a grand view of the open sky.

Vixin leaned her head back and took a breath. A fire sprung to life in the center and she took to watching those hugging and asking questions. Many embraced, some cried, but everyone, it seemed, had something to say to Zak.

She hadn't realized, up until now, just how much they cared for him. It wasn't due to any experience he carried or the way he planned their missions. It had nothing to do with his abilities. It was simply that he cared. Cared for each of them individually, seeing to their needs when others might have turned a blind eye. Others like herself.

He'd taken on a responsibility most would have shied away from and none of his companions took that for granted.

Vixin took another breath, closed her eyes, and found herself drifting. The voices lifted and fell, most lost to her ears until Anton shouted loud enough for the world to hear, "To the woman who saved us all!"

Vixin cracked one eye open, hoping they were referring to someone else, but every eye in the room had locked onto her seated form. Zak was at her side a moment later, offering his hand with a gentle smile on his face.

Daniel stepped forward, his hulking form blocking out the firelight. "If it weren't for you coming to save our sorry asses, we'd have been done for. Everyone chased you two out thus," he pointed to those seated behind Sam, "we were able to make our escape. Thank you."

She tsked but couldn't hide her smile. "Just don't make a habit out of it."

Everyone laughed and Vixin let Zak haul her to her feet and his hand settled on her back. Zak's warmth soaked through her shirt, easing some of the tension from her shoulders. They listened to the others tell their side of the story, likely exaggerating most of it, then she looked at Zak and found him staring right back at her.

Vixin's breath hitched. There was that look again. The same one he'd had at the pond. Her pulse quickened and Vixin's eyes dropped to his lips before darting back to his eyes. She tried to swallow, but somehow her throat had gone dry.

"We have a problem." Blitz stumbled from the cavern entrance. A blush crept up her neck and she was almost grateful for the distraction. "They tracked us."

"Put out the fire," Vixin hissed. Water doused the flames and Vixin spun to Zak. "Chill it, and the ground, make it seem as if no one was here." He obeyed and Vixin pointed toward a back exit she'd spotted earlier. "Everyone in. Now."

"What good—"

She whirled on Anton. "I. Said. Now."

They gathered up what was left of their belongings and filed into the tunnels. She didn't know whether it'd lead them out or to a dead end, but that didn't matter. The only thing that mattered was hiding because not one of them had the strength to fight.

Zak shoved his comrades through one by one, urging them to keep quiet. She lingered by the entrance, eyeing the vines that hung from the hole in the roof.

Vixin reached for her magic. It singed her, stinging from the inside, but she didn't recoil from the pain. Instead, Vixin breathed life into the foliage, commanding it to grow along the walls. She found the tiniest of seeds and sprouted them all, making it look as though a human hadn't touched this place in a millennium.

Footprints were soon covered by ferns and thick, woody branches concealed the exit she gazed out from. As long as no one had a degree in botany they wouldn't notice the shrubs that grew where sunlight never touched.

"What now?" Zak whispered.

Voices sounded at the main entrance and Vixin's only response was to take Zak's hand and move further into the tunnel. She grew plants in their wake, sprinkling in a few that would ensure their pursuers never saw the light of day again.

VIXIN EMERGED from the cave, shielding her eyes from the afternoon sun. Days. They'd been in the dark for days.

She slumped to the ground and her stomach clenched, sending a painful spike through her body. Thanks to Zak, they'd had water, but since losing their packs, no one had eaten, nor had they slept more than a few hours. She'd give every last drop of magic in her body for a good night's rest.

"What's the plan?" someone called. She didn't have the energy to look up.

"We keep moving," Zak said. "And find our way back to the second realm."

Vixin groaned with the rest of them. If they kept moving like this, she just might let their enemies capture her and put her out of her misery. No one looked like they had the energy left to take another step, let alone retrace their way back around the rocky pass.

"Have you ever thought about settling down?" she asked.

Silence stretched before Zak responded, "How would we go about ensuring no one turns our profession against us?" Zak asked.

She stretched her legs out in front of her. "We set up differently, maybe in the trees, somewhere less prone to attack." Zak slumped against the tree across from her and Vixin continued. "I don't know about you, but I'm exhausted and judging from the silence I'd say they are too. We just don't have the energy to make it back to the second realm without recuperating."

"We have friends there."

"You're willing to put our fates in the hands of someone else? What happens if they turn us away? We'd be left tired, hungry, and more vulnerable than ever."

Sam spoke up. "She has a point."

"We can hunt for food, you can get us clean water, and once we find a suitable location, we can build a shelter."

"And how will we know it's the right place to set up?"

Vixin jerked her thumb behind her. "As long as it's far away from those bastards, I don't care where it is. Until then, we survive and take it one day at a time, starting with a halfway decent meal."

Daniel chimed in. "Once we settle, we could hit one more target, somewhere not as well guarded, just to replenish supplies."

Vixin nodded. "And after that, we make our own living. No more runs. We'll wait it out, just like you wanted and once someone reaches the final realm, we'll all go home."

Zak furrowed his brow. "You seemed against that idea the first time I brought it up."

Vixin scoffed. "If we headed to the front lines, we'd die. Well, I probably wouldn't, you might stand a chance with a little more training but look around. One little mishap and this happens. They're not ready, they need time to work with their magic, train in using it properly and then if, *if* they can master their abilities, they might just survive."

Zak smirked. "Sounds like you just volunteered yourself as our permanent teacher."

She laughed to herself. "It's not like anyone else can do it."

"It's settled then." Zak rose to his feet. "Food first."

THEY ATE and rested, each individual more exhausted than the last. Four were set to take watch with two rotations throughout the night, but that didn't stop her from setting up a perimeter. It was pitiful really, nothing more than a few vines strung between trees, but enough of her magic lingered in the stems to alert her if anything tripped over them during the night.

The magic still roared against her, stinging as if she'd disturbed a nest of insects, but she had to keep them safe. Had to keep Zak safe.

Vixin used a twig to draw her plans in the dirt. She carved the details in the soil and sprouted tiny seeds where trees would serve as their salvation.

Above ground, yes, that would be the safest bet. There were so many ways to hide, so many traps she could lay to ensure people didn't dare intrude.

The sprouts shifted, twisting around themselves to form little houses among the branches. They stretched and connected with bridges and ropes that would lead from one level to the next.

Vixin lost herself in the design of a particular house, forming tiny windows high above the others. A rope was the only thing that would lead to her domain and thorns would wrap around the entirety of it to ward against unwanted guests.

"That's some model."

Vixin jolted, a part of her brain seeming to wake up.

Zak pointed to the house she'd created in detail. "I suppose that's to be your fortress of solitude?"

Vixin smirked. "It'll keep you out."

"Oh, I'll find a way."

She scoffed. "Good luck. Unfortunately for you, my father tau—" Her breath hitched when he sat beside her, his body so close she could feel the heat radiating from his skin. Her face ignited and her throat went dry. Why did he always affect her like this?

Vixin kept her gaze forward and took a moment to steady her voice. "Where would you have yours?"

She could feel his gaze burning through her, but instead of pushing, he shifted his attention to her little figurine. "Beside yours of course."

"So you can spy on me?"

"So I can keep you safe."

Vixin rolled her eyes. "I'm perfectly capable of caring for myself. I don't need—"

Her heart leapt as Zak's hand lightly brushed the hair away from her face and lingered on her shoulder. Vixin's pulse pounded in her ears and she finally met his gaze.

Can I? His eyes seemed to ask.

Zak leaned toward her and somehow her body leaned back, closing the distance. She could taste the hot air between them now, could almost—

"Zak, we need you—"

Vixin pulled away, hiding the red blotches she could already feel rising to the surface.

Sam averted his gaze, suddenly interested in the night sky. "Um, sorry, I uh. Actually, it can wait."

Zak huffed. "You're already here, what is it?" Vixin couldn't bring herself to look at Sam and instead focused her attention on the little model she'd created. Or tried to. With her heart racing the way it was, Vixin wasn't sure she could focus on anything but the proximity of the young man who'd almost—

Sam cleared his throat. "We wanted to run the hunting rounds by you."

Vixin released her breath. Right, there were more important things than her raging teenage hormones. For a few fleeting moments she'd forgotten they were on the run, without a home or food.

"Go ahead," she said. "I'm not going anywhere."

Reluctantly, Zak stood, gave her a last lingering look and followed Sam. She laid back in the grass and her breathing returned to normal. A cool breeze ruffled the trees and the heat in her cheeks dissipated.

Vixin kept trying to convince herself this wasn't the time or place to be having such feelings. But if not now, when? When could she explore something beyond the bounds of friendship? When they were safe? Judging from everything she'd already experienced, safety was a long way off.

Vixin counted the long minutes until Zak's return. He paused before her, but she didn't open her eyes. "I'm not asleep if that's what you're wondering."

He sighed and sat down on the other side of her mini model. "You probably should be." She didn't comment. "About earlier."

"Don't worry about it." The lure of sweet darkness was close now. Her body had become one with the ground, her mind drifting with the foggy images behind her eyelids.

Vixin faintly heard Zak chuckle. “In the morning then.”

8

THE GIRL AND MONSTERS

Rain, rain, and more rain. It'd soaked through every pore in her body. Even at night, she couldn't completely escape. A fire only served to dry the outer layers and with the fear of pursuers, they didn't have time to stop for anything more than food and some light rest.

Zak hadn't made another move on her and Vixin couldn't decide if it were due to the miserable weather or their current situation. Truthfully, she was grateful. Between the hunger, cold, and bugs she might have bitten his head off.

Vixin heard the water long before she saw the raging current. Those at the front of the line collapsed in the wet grass. Some pulled out food, eating sodden meat and edible plants. They were losing hope, too tired to see the end was near.

Vixin stalked past them and stood at the river's edge. It rolled and roared, licking her shoes with the promise of a watery death.

She steadied herself and ran an invisible hand over her magic. It no longer stung, but something still fought against her, as if it were warning her that it wasn't quite ready. She grasped it anyway and twisted the power that flowed through her veins down through her feet and into the earth.

She searched the seedlings, taking hold of the sturdiest plants before dragging them through the mud. They sprouted, rising up and up and up until they bent from the weight and collapsed into the water. Those around her gasped and many stood, questions passing between them.

The current yanked at her creation, threatening to pull it from her grasp, but Vixin rooted the vines into the rocky bottom, digging for a foothold deep in the earth. Her plants crawled among the stones, anchoring themselves along the way before emerging on the other side. She rooted the ends into the earth, took a breath, and lifted.

The plants grew, rising above the current to give them safe passage.

The four people in their group able to use earth magic joined her, weaving their power into the anchor points on land. If they'd had carts or horses, she knew the bridge wouldn't have held.

Vixin tottered, but Sam grabbed her elbow. She bristled at the touch, almost outright recoiled, but caught herself. "Hang in there," was all he said before heading across the makeshift bridge.

Each eyed her, most reluctant to step foot on the swaying structure and she didn't blame them. The way the current swirled and raged was enough to make even her skin crawl.

Vixin crossed after Zak and upon hitting the muddy bank on the opposite shore, she released her hold. Instantly, the bridge collapsed, and the river swallowed it like a starving animal.

She let a slow smile creep to her lips. Despite the misery of the rain, it had covered their tracks and now a river separated them from their enemy. It was just a matter of time now.

That night, they found a patch of trees and nestled against the trunks. No one bothered with a shelter, and most only removed their shoes to massage waterlogged skin.

Vixin studied their surroundings and let her gaze linger on the meadow beyond. Not a single light shone from within the darkness. She knew they needed to scout the area, ensure potential neighbors were a long way off, but she'd had enough of the rain and cold.

Vixin coaxed her magic into four trees. Those seated against them yelped in surprise, but she paid them no mind as she walked toward their center.

The trees grew and grew until their canopy blotted out the moonless sky. She let the branches tangle together then slithered vines halfway up the trunks. They circled to create a thick knot before reaching toward one another, intertwining and thickening until not a single drop of water hit those beneath it.

The four able to use earth mimicked her actions, growing the trees along the outside edges to a similar height before expanding the middle platform.

Moments later a fire started, then shirts, shoes, and even pants were hung to dry. Vixin averted her gaze as Anton went a bit too wild, but she couldn't stop the smile his carefree attitude brought to her face.

"Going soft on me?" Zak tugged off a shoe.

"Maybe I'm just sick of the rain."

"Ah, so selfishness caused you to take pity on them."

"Exactly." They both laughed.

"Seriously though, do you think we're far enough away?"

"I won't know anything until we've scouted the perimeter, but the rain washed away our tracks days ago and with a river separating us, I'd say we're as good as we're gonna get."

Zak looked up. "So, we're really going to live in the trees huh?"

"It'll ensure we're ready if anyone does come for us."

He eyed her. "You look ready to fall over."

Her head was swimming, and her magic had tried warning her, stinging its way through her veins like an angry hornet. "I might have overdone it."

"You still haven't recovered?"

"Creating perimeters every night kinda prevents that."

"Every night? Vixin we've been moving for over a week."

"I'm aware."

He stared at her. "So much for only looking out for number one."

"I guess your bad habits are rubbing off on me."

Zak chuckled. "Come on, if anyone deserves to dry off, I think it's you."

She followed him and when Zak placed an arm around her shoulders, she didn't push him away.

VIXIN DIDN'T rest. She built, creating paths and archways that weaved themselves between the trees. Thick trunks twisted around one another to serve as pillars that reached toward a second story.

Vixin leaned against a trunk, allowing her magic to settle. The stinging had grown more painful by the hour, but there was still a lot to get done before she could allow herself rest.

She watched those running back and forth on the ground and wondered what would happen when she finally finished. Was she content to live a simple life while someone else tackled the hard part? It might be fun to test her abilities in a different way.

"You know, that wicked grin prevents you from making friends." Zak handed her a steaming cup. "Do I even want to know?"

"Probably not, you wouldn't approve."

He leaned against the opposite wall she'd been working on. It didn't have a roof yet, nor anything in its center, but once she finished, it'd be a sturdy home.

"Sticking around to enjoy the boring life?"

She took a drink. "What makes you say that?"

Zak patted the wall behind him. "You've been working on this all morning. I assumed it was for you."

Vixin averted her gaze. "Actually, it's yours."

Zak stared at her then turned to study the wall. He walked a few paces to his right and craned his neck to view the branches she'd been forming above.

Zak point. "You're really going to make yourself climb all the way up there?"

"It'll be good for me. Besides, I can't have anyone sneaking in on me in the middle of the night, now can I?"

"And if they try?"

She took another drink. "Let's hope Sam can get to them before the toxin sets in."

Zak gave an exasperated sigh. "What's with women and poison?"

She shrugged. "I suppose it's in our genes. Just like men and their swords." Zak chuckled and they both turned toward those running back and forth below.

"You won't get bored?"

"With what?"

"The simple life. Skipping out on adventures that could get us killed."

"Last I checked, we still have at least one to tackle."

He smiled. "Right, but after that. Am I going to wake up one day and wonder where you ran off to?"

"Have I given that impression?"

"Not recently. I just want you to know that I'm not the only one who'd miss you. Sam doesn't shut up about you either."

Vixin clicked her tongue. "Well, if Sam wants to keep his arms intact, he'll keep his distance."

"You haven't broken mine yet." Zak brushed the hair away from her shoulder.

"Yet," she emphasized and gave him a playful smile. "So, about this last run."

"No need to worry, I already have a team on it. They'll be back in a few days, we'll make a plan, then presto, we're set."

"Good, because I need new clothes."

"And furniture," he added.

Vixin barked out a laugh. "Plan to carry a couch out now?" She gestured him inside his new home and tugged at the vines in the floor. They rose, twisting around one another until a loveseat formed in the corner. “There, all you need now are cushions.”

Vixin turned, but Zak was there. Close. Too close. His breath hit her face and her stomach twisted in knots. Zak’s hand grazed her cheek with a feather-like touch. “Would you really break my arm?”

Vixin slowly shook her head, not trusting herself to form words. Her mind raced as Zak leaned in and—

“Zak, how long are you going to laze out on me up here?” Sam called from outside the door. Vixin sidestepped before Sam entered and she could have sworn she heard Zak growl. “Come on man, you’re the one who said we had work to get done.”

Zak gave her an apologetic look. “Yeah, yeah, I’m coming.”

DAYS PASSED with Zak’s assurance that whoever he’d sent out on the scouting mission could more than handle themselves. After their last encounter, she wasn’t so sure.

Vixin glanced at the horizon line and signed, tugging at her magic to patch the final hole in her roof. She inched her way down the steep slope, then dropped off the side, grabbing the ledge to swing herself through the large window.

A fresh breeze filtered through, hitting the sweat on her face as she stood in the circular space. Sure, windows meant someone could sneak in, but she had measures in place to ensure they never made it out again.

She’d placed her home high above the others with a single vine dangling from a hole on the outskirts of the floor. Zak had shaken his head at it, but it wasn’t as though she wanted visitors anyway.

Vixin circled the open space, the inside still completely barren as she contemplated what she’d like to find within.

Flowers. She decided.

Elaborate flowers that would thrive and fill the entire room with a fragrance sweeter than honey. She'd start with one of her favorites.

The vines crawled their way from the ground, twisting around the structures below before reaching out from the branches that surrounded her domain. They crawled in through the windows and around her roof before the long, blue flowers budded and blossomed one by one.

The sweet aroma filling the air reminded her of a porch her and her father had sat upon in the early spring. One of their former homes in Ohio.

She'd never miss the winters there, even if it did bring its own pleasantries and vaguely wondered if they'd get deep snows here or if the climate would stay relatively warm. They were supposedly in some sort of simulation after all.

A game. She still couldn't quite wrap her head around the concept, hadn't had much time to consider the idea really. But whether they were in the real world or a fake one, her goal remained the same. Survive and get home. That was all that mattered in the end.

"These should be wrapped around every house." Zak reached for the flower then hesitated.

Vixin giggled. "You can touch that one."

A sly smile crossed his face as he brushed his hands across the delicate flowers. "Have to check, never know with you."

"You should consider yourself lucky, I could be playing for the other team." She sauntered toward him. "And trust me when I say, you wouldn't have escaped my traps."

"Not sure if that's supposed to scare or comfort me."

"Both." Vixin tilted her head. "How did you get in here anyway?"

He pointed toward her trapdoor. "Climbed."

She raised her brows. "Wow. Didn't realize you had it in you."

"After all the hell you've put us through, you didn't think I could climb a rope?"

"Rope climbing isn't just about strength." She pointed a finger at him. "You've had practice."

He shrugged. "Nothing like you've had. Though I do hold the school record for the fastest climb."

"They have records for that?"

"I live in a small town."

"Well then Mr. Champion. Care to take on a challenger?"

IT BECAME a game. Who could climb the vines the fastest? Vixin had woven two vines around the second-floor railing and let them dangle to the ground.

Not even Zak had been able to keep up with her. He'd come close, close enough that her forearms had burnt from the exertion, but after reaching the top and dangling from a branch with careless abandon, Zak had declared her the winner.

She'd joked about visiting his school to steal his crown, but Zak had only smiled, stating he'd be happy just to see her in the outside world.

Vixin's gaze lingered on the horizon. It'd been four days.

"They should have been back by now," Zak said.

"Should we send out a search party?"

"I'd hate to spread us any thinner than we already are. Daniel is careful, he wouldn't do anything reckless."

"Maybe they're lying low somewhere or trying to shake someone off their trail."

"Maybe."

Vixin crossed her arms. "No sense in worrying about it now. They'll get back when they get back. At least we know our enemies aren't close."

"Or they're too close."

Vixin cringed. "I could set up a perimeter, one that would one hundred percent ensure we aren't caught by surprise."

"And risk killing our friends?" Vixin didn't comment. Zak sighed.

"A perimeter would be good, just, nothing that could kill anyone."

Zak paced down the walkway, running his hands through his hair before locking his fingers behind his head. He wasn't the only one worried.

Vixin let her magic glide through the trees and into the earth. She gathered seeds, transporting them to form a protective circle beneath and around their camp. She'd make it so that if anyone did come for them, it'd be the last thing they'd ever do.

VIXIN SPROUTED another tree from the muddy ground. The rain had eased up, but still came far too frequently for her liking. At least it kept the river swollen.

Someone called from above, indicating for a branch to be extended. She complied and smiled to herself. At one time she might have told them all to figure it out on their own. But now they treated her like one of their own. Like family.

Zak had gotten what he wanted after all.

Vixin's adrenaline spiked with the distant scream that echoed across the plains. She jumped to her feet, eyes scanning until she locked onto four figures running through the tall grass as if their lives depended on it.

Zak sprinted through the trees and into the open meadow before she made it to ground level. Five others followed; the rest stunned into silence.

Vixin's stomach dropped, her heart skidding to a halt with it.

There are other things out there. Monsters, creatures like you've never seen.

She'd thought it'd been a ploy to keep her around. A scare tactic like the ones parents used to keep their children in line. She never imagined…

Her blood chilled when the beast jumped, clamping its powerful jaw around the slowest runner. Its friends joined the frenzy, ripping and tearing flesh while the young man screamed and screamed and screamed.

She let out a shuddering breath. She'd read. She'd studied. Hell, she'd killed, but this? Flesh torn from bone, blood dripping from the canines of a wolf. No… not a wolf. Something darker, something bigger, with more teeth and—a monster. And Zak was headed right for it.

"Stop!" No one listened. "Zak, I said stop!"

He swiveled, his body still moving toward the creatures as he gave her a frantic, pleading look. Those around him paused, glancing between her and their leader.

Vixin knelt, her arms shaking as she dug her fingers into the dirt. Her magic fanned out, seeking the seeds she'd buried around the perimeter. If their comrades could just get over that invisible line…

Another beast leapt through the air, sinking its teeth into their friend's shoulder. His screams flooded her heart with a heaviness Vixin wasn't sure she could bear.

Zak started running again, but Vixin shouted, "Zak, wait!"

"I can't just let them—"

"Trust me!"

His look of helplessness tore through her like a hot blade. It was the same look he'd given her the day he thought she'd be tortured. His desperate gaze kept shooting between her and the two men running for their lives.

They were tired. Slowing, but Vixin willed them on.

Just a little further.

She gripped the blades of grass in her fists.

Come on, a little further.

Almost.

Their feet crossed the line and Vixin's magic ripped from the ground like a wild beast. Vines plunged into the creatures still charging and their howls of rippling pain echoed as monster after monster impaled themselves upon thorns as large as her arm.

Vixin screamed, letting her rage soak into the earth. Her magic grew in a wide arch, catching those attempting to circle around her structure. She kept pulling, shifting the plants this way and that.

This was *her* home.

This was *her* family.

And she'd be damned if she let this world take them away from her.

Ice spread along the ground, carving a path for their friends as it sailed toward the few creatures she'd missed. Vixin didn't let up and their magic collided with the monsters together, blood dripping from both vine and ice.

One of their companions tripped, but Vixin wrapped them in a thorny cocoon before the creatures could claim them. Zak's magic slammed through two beasts before crawling along her wall to solidify the barrier.

Their comrades, who'd been silent until now, charged into the fray. Their magic wasn't as strong, but with pinpointed accuracy they could eliminate the remaining threats.

And they did.

Silence stretched across the field and a soft whine started somewhere within the thorns. She relished in its suffering, whatever it was.

Vixin's breathing turned short and shallow. Blood pulsed in her ears as she stood in the aftermath. Her eyes traced the long wall of thorns and her body trembled.

Bodies hung in the air like trophies, their blood either dripping to the earth, or rolling down near-translucent spikes of ice.

Zak used the hilt of his sword to break through the sphere guarding their friends. They emerged, shaken but safe.

Her breath wouldn't calm. Her body wouldn't stop shaking.

"Are you hurt?" Sam stood a few paces away, his brows scrunched together as he looked her over. "Vixin, can—"

9

THE GIRL AND A PLAN

Warmth flooded her body. Too much warmth. And her bones ached so deep she thought she could feel it in her very soul. It was a part of her that hadn't existed before this world. This terrible, wretched, confusing world.

Vixin opened her eyes to a starry void. A fire crackled to her left and Zak sat against the tree to her right. He gazed into the night, looking just as exhausted as she felt.

She shifted to sit up and Zak was there before she could protest. "Easy does it."

Blood rushed through her head and she leaned against him until the dizzy spell passed. "I'm all right."

"That's the second time you've passed out on me. Not sure that counts as all right."

"I just pushed it too far. Again." She pressed a finger to her temple, trying to rub away the pounding headache. "I'm sorry, I wish I could have done something sooner."

"Don't be sorry. You saved two men, along with the rest of us."

Vixin examined the faces surrounding them. Six in total, all circled around the fire. "Maybe we should head up, it'd be safer."

Zak nodded and helped her stand. Her legs trembled, but Zak held her tight, tighter than he ever had. He nodded to someone and vines wrapped around their torsos. It felt strange to be lifted by magic that wasn't her own.

She reached inward and hissed when her magic bit back.

"What's wrong?"

"Nothing, just sore."

"Do I need to get Sam?"

Vixin shook her head. "Just take me somewhere quiet."

Zak nodded and kept his arm around her as they hobbled down the pathway. Vixin glued her eyes to the ground, afraid she'd find someone with enough sorrow in their gaze to ignite her own.

Vixin hardly noticed where they walked until Zak turned into his home. He led her to the small couch she'd constructed days ago and sat her down before starting a fire in the opposite corner.

He didn't say much, and part of Vixin wondered if Zak wanted her around right now. "Did you," she paused, almost afraid to ask. "Did you ever lose anyone before I came along?"

The fire caught and he threw in some kindling. "One, but it wasn't anyone's fault." She waited, the small fire growing in its stone hearth. "He took his own life. It happened after we saw our first horde of monsters and barely escaped. The fear of being eaten alive consumed him and we found him with his wrists slit the following morning."

Zak took a breath. "None of this is your fault. We knew the risks when we started, we just never thought…it's hard you know? Seeing someone die when that person is someone you care for."

Vixin stared at the fire then looked at her hands. "Do you think staying away from the frontlines is the best thing to do?"

"Like you said, they're not strong enough to fight."

"But we are. We could offer our services in exchange for their protection. Safety in numbers and all that. Even if I teach them, no one can learn everything overnight." She sighed. "They all hesitated today. It's hard to admit, but they're not cut out for this."

"Are any of us? I will protect them. We'll build bigger walls, set stronger traps, fortify ourselves until even those battling on the frontlines wouldn't dare mess with us."

"Sounds like you're going to need a lot of help."

"Yours is all I need. If you're willing to stick around."

Vixin locked eyes with him. Sadness lingered there, so deep it almost swallowed her whole. "I'm not going anywhere."

Zak sat beside her and held his arm up. "Come here, and don't worry, I don't exactly have the energy to deal with a broken arm right now."

Vixin gave him a small smile and curled her body against his, resting her head on his chest. She listened to his heart for a long while, watching the flames shift to embers. She gazed into those red coals until her eyes grew heavy and her body fell into a deep, dreamless sleep.

VIXIN EXAMINED their handy work from outside Zak's hut. A barrier of trees two-foot high encircled their camp now. Trees that would contain traps for their enemies once they were fully grown.

She shouldered a pack. By the time her and Zak returned, the trees would likely be close to ten feet. That was her hope at least. The sooner they got a proper barrier in place, the sooner they could put the bulk of their worries behind them.

Vixin jumped when she turned to find Sam staring at her from the doorway. "I couldn't talk him out of it," he took several steps toward her, "and I doubt I'll be able to talk you out of it either, so," he stopped mere inches from her and Vixin tried not to bristle. "Promise me something. Promise you'll take care of him and if things get out of hand, that you won't leave him behind."

Her lips parted. "What makes you think I'd ever abandon him?"

Sam angled his body to the side, rubbing at the back of his neck.

"You just don't—you're kind of a hardass and if he puts himself in a situation that seems hopeless…"

"You're afraid I'd leave him." Vixin tried to hide her disappointment. "Despite what you may believe, I'd never abandon Zak."

"And the rest of us?"

She tilted her head and attempted a playful smile. "No promises."

"I still don't agree with you two going alone."

"We told you—"

"Yeah, yeah, it'll be easier to sneak in, I get it."

"We've done it before."

"And gotten caught," he reminded her. Sam took a breath. "Do you have everything you need?"

"Hey Vixin, are you—" Zak paused just inside the doorway. His gaze flickered between her and Sam and something like surprise flashed across his face. "Are you ready?"

She patted her bag, glanced at Sam and said. "I think I got it covered." Then slid past Zak and into the evening.

10

THE GIRL AND AN ADVENTURE

Vixin and Zak walked for several hours, trekking across the meadow, past small clusters of trees, and finally into a thickly wooded area. The two who'd survived the scouting mission had reported a civilization beyond the trees. A place where they just might be able to tackle one last job.

Zak was unusually quiet, his gaze diverting from hers whenever she looked his way. She figured he'd just been thinking of the two young men who'd lost their lives.

With nightfall, they set up camp and Vixin fanned her magic out to set up a perimeter.

"You did it again, didn't you?"

Vixin inclined her head. "Did what?"

"Set up a barrier around us."

"Of course."

"I could learn," he offered, "So you wouldn't have to do it every night."

"You'd exhaust yourself trying."

Silence encompassed them again. "How long have you and Sam been talking?"

"Jealous?" Zak opened his mouth and closed it again and Vixin burst out laughing. "Is that why you've been so quiet?"

"I just don't want to push if—"

"He was worried about you." Vixin folded her arms behind her head. "Asked me to keep an eye out is all."

"So you two?"

She huffed, though still found him amusing. "I've never been involved with anyone."

"Ever?"

Vixin's face grew warm as she realized what she'd said. "I already told you I didn't have friends, what makes you think I'd have a boyfriend?"

"Right, I forgot, you like learning to kick ass and there's no time for anything else."

Vixin glared at him. "Not everyone needs other people to define their worth. Some of us are happy being our introverted little selves surrounded by books and music."

"Music?"

"Contrary to what you might believe, I don't spend all my time training."

Zak scooted closer, the brightness to his smile returning. She vaguely wondered how hurt he would have been if she had chosen Sam.

"Do you play?"

"Occasionally."

He cocked his head, "Are you going to tell me what?"

She sighed. "Since you'll likely pester me until I do, piano. Since I was four."

"And you've never been with a guy?"

"Not sure how that relates to music."

"Just curious."

She gave him a devilish grin. "I can still break your arm."

"Trust me, I know."

"Your turn, you ever been with a girl?"

Color rose to Zak's cheeks and he averted his gaze. "Once."

"Someone waiting for you back home?"

He shook his head. "Nothing like that. It was a few years ago."

"And?"

"I was fifteen. We were stupid and after spending an entire month afraid she was pregnant, she broke it off."

"Did you like her?"

"Not enough for that level of commitment. I wouldn't have abandoned her, but I don't think either of us would have been happy in the long run."

"You guys still talk?"

He shook his head. "She avoided me after we split and then moved the following year. Something about her dad and a job."

"What was it that made you like her?"

Zak flushed. "I don't know. Why?"

"Just trying to figure out why you feel that way about me."

"I, um, I don't know. You're easy to talk to I guess."

"Most would disagree with you."

"I just mean you're real. You don't try to be something that you're not. I guess I just...like that."

Vixin curled up next to their small fire. She stared at Zak and Zak stared at her. Two kids thrown into the trenches of hell and expected to survive. Together. They could tackle anything as long as they were together.

A TUG on her magic jolted Vixin awake. A stick cracked, someone cursed, and Vixin was on her feet, daggers drawn before Zak even registered there was a threat.

Vixin wrapped her magic around their bodies and lifted them into the treetops. She slowed her breathing, straining to listen. Dawn approached, but she didn't have enough light to see the features of the men who stomped through their camp.

One of them kicked the fire, sending embers soaring through the air. "We know you're out there," he called. "We're not here to harm anyone." He paused, waiting for a reply. Vixin held still as his eyes scanned the trees and passed right over their hiding place.

"We saw the fire," he continued, "and thought you might need help." Another pause. "You're welcome to come with us. We have food, water, shelter."

This might be easier than she thought.

Vixin let a few seconds pass before she responded in the feeblest voice she could manage. "Do we have your word? That you won't hurt us?"

Zak gave her a desperate, confused look, but she winked at him and he nodded his understanding.

The man lifted empty hands. "You have my word."

Vixin grabbed a vine and slid from the tree with Zak following suit. She ducked behind him, placing her palms against his back.

The bastard fell for it hook, line, and sinker.

"Just the two of you?" She nodded. "You're lucky to be alive. You have magic at least, right?" Fishing for information already.

Vixin prodded Zak's back and Zak replied. "I have a bit."

The stranger peeked around Zak as if he were trying to get a good look at her. "There's no reason to be scared. Come with us and we'll get you settled in." Vixin eyed their wrists, but they'd hidden their stones from view. "What's your name?"

"Zak." He took a step forward and shook the stranger's hand. "And this is Vixin."

"Sister?"

"Friend."

He smiled, though it didn't quite reach his eyes. "She's very lucky to have found you. Well, it's best not to linger. A hot meal is waiting if you care to join us." She gave Zak an affirmative squeeze.

"That sounds wonderful."

Their leader, Rolfe, bombarded Zak with questions as morning shifted to afternoon. He lied with ease, forming a story that even she might have believed. When Rolfe directed the questions at her, Vixin dodged with the guise of a shy demeanor. A lamb who'd scarcely missed the slaughter.

The group of nine stopped for lunch and Rolfe kindly shared meat from his pack. She devoured it as if she hadn't eaten in days, as did Zak. It was part of their story. Two lost souls wondering if they'd ever be safe again.

Just before nightfall, Vixin spotted their camp. A wall surrounded it, like many others, and sentinels patrolled the exits. She hadn't been worried until now.

They were too alert, just like their last hit. And if their last encounter was anything to go by…

Vixin exchanged a nervous glance with Zak whose gaze lingered on the guards stationed by the front gate.

"Slim pickings this time?" A man called from the top.

Rolfe shrugged. "They can't all be winners." What the hell did that mean?

The heavy gate closed behind them and Vixin followed Rolfe through the town. Zak kept close, the nervousness in his gaze far from faked. She took in details, labeling each landmark as something that might help or hinder.

Rolfe led them into a large, three-story building and headed straight for the stairs. Her stomach grumbled with the smell of food. Hopefully they'd live up to that promise at least.

He opened a door on the third floor and gestured them inside. The smell of musty sheets hit her and Vixin resisted the urge to recoil.

"Weapons." Rolfe held out his hand.

"Why?" Zak asked.

"We can't have armed strangers in our midst."

She took a tentative step behind Zak and pulled a dagger from beneath his shirt. Vixin stuffed it up her sleeve. "Will we get them back?"

"Not my call."

Zak unbuckled his sword belt. "I thought we were coming here as allies, not prisoners."

Rolfe smirked. "You'll have to prove yourselves first. Obey and we'll see about letting you walk around freely."

"Obey?"

"You'll have your orders shortly."

Vixin handed Zak her weapons and, in turn, Zak handed them to Rolfe. He eyed the two before slamming the door. A click followed a second later.

Zak threw up his arms. "Well that could have gone better."

Vixin shushed him and pressed her ear against the door. She waited until Rolfe's footsteps retreated.

"I assume you have a plan?"

Vixin shrugged. "No need for us to sneak past the guards now."

"Right, did you intend on getting our weapons taken too?"

"No, but we have other weapons they don't know about."

Zak crossed his arms. "So. The plan?"

"We buy in and play the part. I'll locate their warehouse tomorrow and come nightfall, we'll be out of here before they even know what hit them."

"And how do you plan on sneaking out with the supplies?"

"You just let me worry about that."

ROLFE CAME for her and Zak before sunrise. Neither had slept and though she'd given Zak all the assurance she could offer, he still didn't like the idea of them being separated.

It was inevitable.

The guards ushered them out the door, gruff, but not violent. It was there that one took her by the arm and led her right, while Rolfe escorted Zak to the left. He gave her a worried glance, but she offered a shy smile in return. It was only until tonight.

Vixin allowed the guard to escort her by the arm, playing the ever-submissive female. She'd like to find him later and give him a friendly reminder to keep his hands to himself.

Calm. Focus. Control.

She could do this. Less than twelve hours and she'd be free to do as she pleased.

Vixin's stomach grumbled as they passed the bakery, but her appetite quickly disappeared when they entered the next room and the smell of days old sweaty clothes hit her full in the face.

She coughed and struggled not to gag.

"Maria, find her work to do."

A woman in her thirties took Vixin by her other arm and guided her to a washtub. Maria gave her a quick rundown of her tasks and disappeared behind a line of hanging garments.

Vixin stared at the dirty water and the things floating within.

One day.

She took a breath, grabbed a brush, and pinched the ends of a soiled shirt. This had to be the worst day of her life.

VIXIN PEEKED her head from behind the doors. Most of the other women were cleaning up, but she'd finished an hour ago. She eyed the fresh bread and stew at the stall next door.

After a quick glance, Vixin snuck from the entrance and grabbed a bowl from the large serving table. She stuffed a piece of bread in her shirt and another in her mouth. It melted and she couldn't stifle the moan that escaped her lips. Sam needed this recipe.

Vixin scanned the area, looking over each person, trailer, and box. A man opened a large swinging door and she glimpsed weapons lining the walls before he closed it again. Bingo.

"Hey, what are you doing out here?" The same guard from earlier ripped the bowl from her hands. She stared at the ground even though every instinct in her wanted to claw his eyes out.

"I'm sorry. I was hungry."

"People who leave early don't eat." She didn't respond. "You'll work twice as hard tomorrow, then we'll talk about food."

Asshole.

Despicable lowlife, picking on a seemingly innocent girl. If Zak weren't somewhere in the compound, she might have blown their cover right there.

"I'm sorry." She donned the face of a meek girl. The very girl her father had trained out of her. She'd never be weak, never be like the women surrounding her.

He grunted and led her back to their room without the offer of a bath. Zak was already pacing by the time she arrived.

He let out a long breath upon seeing her. "You all right?"

Vixin nodded and let the guard leave the room before looking him over. His boots sat in the corner, covered in mud and the redness in his hands told her they'd assigned him to hard labor.

"What'd they have you doing?"

"Cutting logs to reinforce the wall." His gaze roamed over her. "And you?"

"I don't want to talk about it." She reached inside her shirt. "But I did steal you a present." Zak's eyes lit up upon seeing the loaf.

"Did you find anything else?"

"Yep."

"And?"

"I'm not staying to work double duty tomorrow."

11

THE GIRL AND HAPPINESS

Vixin slipped the knife in her boot and climbed out the third story window. She shimmied along the narrow ledge and heard a string of curses as Zak followed.

Both froze when a pair of guards passed below, then Vixin dropped herself onto a beam and slid to the ground. She pressed her body against the nearest wall then whistled the all clear for Zak to follow.

They could do this. She'd snuck into a hundred places before being pulled into this crazy world and she hadn't had magic back then. She idly wondered what her father would make of this. If he'd be proud of her actions and reactions.

The pair of them rounded another building and Vixin stopped dead. Two guards stood before her, both with their backs turned. She shifted her gaze to her feet and took two silent steps backward before Zak yanked her behind a wall.

They waited and after what felt like an eternity, the men moved on. She crawled toward the main door of the storehouse to inspect the lock.

Chains. They'd make too much noise and she couldn't afford getting caught.

Vixin pointed toward the back and they crawled along the perimeter.

She checked the first window, then the second.

Vixin knelt and pulled at plants below the surface, shifting the dirt to the side so they could jump through.

She took a final glance at their surroundings then jerked her head toward the hole. Zak gave her a 'you've got to be kidding me' look as he sized up the hole and then himself.

She repressed the urge to giggle as he lowered himself in, then followed, shifting the dirt back in place to cover their tracks.

Inside, Vixin stood, made an attempt at wiping the dirt from her clothes and gave up upon smearing mud across her pants.

"Please tell me your escape plan doesn't involve going underground."

"Brilliant idea, right?"

"And if I'm claustrophobic?"

"Then I guess it's the hard labor life for you."

"You promised Sam you wouldn't leave me behind."

"I won't, but I'd prefer not to waste energy dragging you either."

Zak grimaced and Vixin went to survey the warehouse. She waltzed over to a box and removed the lid to find several high-quality swords and daggers. Perfect. Too bad they couldn't take everything.

She tugged a large blanket out from under a stack of boxes and began lining up everything they could carry. Clothing and weapons were all they needed to ensure a comfortable start.

They were so close now.

Vixin rolled the items up and tied a rope around its center.

"You realize that's going to be heavy."

"It's fine, I'll be dragging it with my magic anyway." A hole opened up between them, large enough for Zak and the pack to fit in. Zak's face went white.

"Are you really scared of small spaces?"

He swallowed. "They're not my favorite."

"Don't worry. I won't let it collapse on us or anything and by morning we'll be back on the surface and forget it ever happened."

"Morning?"

"We have to ensure we're far enough away. Don't want to risk leading them home."

Zak gritted his teeth, took a breath, and dropped in. She followed, tugging the bag behind her and they began their long crawl through the tunnel together.

HOURS LATER Zak cursed and stilled. "This is the worst idea you've ever had."

Vixin paused behind him, digging a rock from her palm. "Really? I thought it was one of my better plans. No deaths, no warning cries, just a quick in and out."

"I guess."

Vixin took a moment to listen to his rapid breathing. If she had to guess, his heart was probably pounding along with it. She hadn't even considered the possibility of claustrophobia and hearing the distress in his voice was almost worse than seeing it in his eyes.

"We're almost there," she promised.

"That's what you said an hour ago."

"Actually, it's only been about twenty minutes." He didn't respond, and his breathing came faster. If he didn't slow it down, he was going to hyperventilate.

Vixin crawled forward, dirt falling around her head and placed a hand on his ankle. She slid her way up to his arms, feeling in the dark and finally grabbed his hand.

"You've trusted me this far. There's only a bit more to go. I promise, I won't let this tunnel collapse around you."

He shifted. "And the collapsing behind us?"

"On purpose, so no one can follow."

He took several deep breaths. "I got stuck in a well once, when I was a kid. Broke my leg and sat in the dark for half the night. I was in the trees behind our house, at an old settlement that I wasn't supposed to be playing around."

"Well you're not stuck now, and your leg isn't broken. It's not much further."

Zak took another deep breath. Then another. He squeezed her hand, then scooted from her reach and started down the tunnel again.

In truth, they had at least two hours to go, but she feared telling him that might make him claw his way out then and there. So Vixin kept her mouth shut and followed, dragging the pack behind her and collapsing the tunnel in her wake.

VIXIN HAD never seen someone so happy to breathe fresh air again. Upon declaring their freedom, her magic hadn't moved fast enough, and he'd half clawed his way out, ripping at roots before she could even break the surface.

Zak knelt on the ground for several minutes, staring at their former campsite while she curled greenery around their goods and pulled them from the hole.

Dawn had barely risen. Neither had slept in two days, but they still had a long way to go if they wanted to stay ahead of any pursuers.

"We should keep moving."

Zak let out a heavy sign. "What's the longest you've gone without sleep?"

"Three days."

"And food?"

"I only lasted two with that one." Her stomach growled and Zak's answered. "I'll watch for berries along the way and we'll get fish from the river tonight if your magic is feeling up to it."

"Oh, trust me, I'll make it feel up to it."

Neither talked much as they trudged through the forest and finally into the clearing. Despite her haggard state, Vixin kept an eye on the trees, willing whoever might be following to stop there. She'd been sure to cover their tracks along the way.

"I'm surprised you aren't exhausted after all that digging."

She gave a strangled laugh. "Oh, I am."

"Then we should rest."

"It's not safe."

"What if we crossed the river? We could hide in the trees over there."

"Is your magic strong enough for that?"

"I'm sure I can manage."

Vixin glanced at the raging water and gave Zak a doubtful look. He ignored her and frost crawled from his feet toward the riverbank.

A thin layer of ice formed over the water only to be washed away with the current. Zak furrowed his brow and the ice layered itself again, thickening and spreading across the moving water. Vixin eyed him and then the bridge as a solid wall formed on either side to serve as a rail.

"We should hurry."

The strain in his voice had Vixin propelling herself forward, sliding more than running across the slippery surface. She sprouted plants from the opposite bank to carry their pack then they both headed for a cluster of trees.

Vixin threw their bag to the ground, collapsed against a tree, and closed her eyes. A minute was all she needed. Just enough time to rest her burning eyes before they continued on.

The crackling of a fire startled her awake and Vixin's hand shot to her dagger. She took in Zak, the fish, a fire, and settled back against the tree. "You shouldn't have let me sleep."

He looked at the blade in her hand. "I wasn't very well going to wake you." Zak handed her a roasted fish. "Eat."

"How long was I out?"

"A few hours. Don't worry, I've been keeping an eye on the trees. It doesn't look like anyone is coming for us."

Vixin downed her fish and threw the bones in the fire before snuffing it out. "We've wasted enough time. Let's get home before dark."

"Home?"

"It's the closest thing we have to one right now."

The two crossed the raging water with their combined magic and raced for their destination.

Darkness had settled before they arrived at the ring of trees. They'd grown bigger, thicker. Pretty soon they'd have the trunks so thick, they'd press in on one another and no one would ever find their little piece of paradise.

Four of their comrades sat on watch and Vixin elbowed Zak. "If I had the energy, I'd love to mess with them."

"You'd likely give them all heart attacks and earn us a few broken bones."

Zak stepped forward, took a deep breath and shouted Sam's name as loud as he could. The four on watch scrambled to their feet and Vixin shook her head.

"Subtle."

He shrugged. "I don't want them trying to kill us."

The two walked through the trees and a fire user lit up the area. Upon seeing their faces, everyone relaxed. A rope dropped from the first level and Sam poked his head over the railing. More lights sprang to life from above.

"Zak?"

Zak grinned like a schoolboy and grabbed the rope. He turned to her. "Should I carry you?"

Vixin rolled her eyes and ushered him up. "I'd sooner die."

He made a face before jumping onto the rope. It swung, but Zak wrapped his legs around it and shimmied up. She followed right after, eliciting a cry of outrage from him as she swung them back and forth.

At the top, Zak offered his hand and she took it, easing herself onto the familiar platform.

Sam clasped Zak on the shoulder then pulled him into a friendly embrace.

Vixin did her best to brush the dirt from her clothes. "Safe and sound, just like I promised."

Sam tilted his head. "Did it go well?"

Vixin leaned over the railing and hauled their prize from the ground. She plopped it on the platform at their feet. "More than well."

"Then we should celebrate!"

"It's the middle of the night," Vixin said.

"What are you, my mother? Come on, it'll be fun."

She laughed. "Fine, but where are we holding this celebration?"

"You two go get cleaned up. Leave the rest to me."

VIXIN WASHED her face, changed her clothes, and ran her fingers through her hair before joining Zak on the second level deck.

"They built a dance room while we were gone."

"Because that's more important than the perimeter."

He chuckled. "People need entertainment."

Vixin yawned. "I'd like to entertain my bed."

Zak gave her a sleepy smile. "You and me both." She gawked at him and Zak stared in confusion before turning red. "No, that came out wrong. I meant my bed. Not that, um…"

Vixin laughed. "I think we're both more than a little sleep deprived."

Music sounded from somewhere below and Zak groaned.

"Sounds like Sam has the music going."

"Give it ten minutes and you'll be wishing you'd never heard his voice."

"He sings?"

"If you want to call it that."

12

THE GIRL AND HER FAMILY

Vixin twirled to the music, spinning from person to person as they cheered, laughed, and let themselves get drunk on the melody of freedom. Those seated stomped their boots and the rhythm echoed through her bones.

Someone took her by the hand, spinning her once, twice, before handing her off to another. She vibrated from head to toe wondering what had ever kept her away from the company of friends.

She'd never had anyone until now. Never trusted anyone besides her father.

Those dancing in the open space were her people, her tribe, her family.

Sam took her hand next, and spun her, just as lost in the moment as everyone else. She switched partners again, then exited the dance floor, still clapping as she made her way to a seat.

Vixin poured herself a drink from the pitcher on the table. Lemon water. Her foot bounced as she watched the others dance and Sam tackle a very embarrassing move. She cheered for him, then leaned back in her chair.

"Someone's having fun." Zak sat beside her.

"Why aren't you out there?"

"I'll leave the dance moves to Sam."

"Coward."

Zak shifted to face her and reached a hand out to graze her cheek. Their eyes met and her stomach tightened.

"A coward wouldn't keep running back to you." Her entire body coiled in on itself and heat raced up her neck to color her cheeks. Zak's fingers trailed to the back of her neck and he leaned in. "You can say no."

Their breath mingled, her stomach fluttered, and then Zak's lips met hers and Vixin thought her entire world would implode.

He pulled back slightly, far too soon, but his eyes were searching, waiting.

Yes, or no.

A million thoughts raced through her mind at once, but only one mattered. She wanted Zak. She wanted him to be hers and only hers. She wanted happiness.

Vixin crashed her lips into his, almost toppling their stools. Her fingers reached up to entwine themselves in his hair while his hands circled her back, squeezing her against his chest so hard she wasn't sure she'd ever breathe again.

Their lips moved together, and his tongue traced the inside of her mouth in a way that shattered any shred of control she might have had.

"Get a room!"

Vixin broke from the embrace breathless and heated.

Zak waved a hand to shoo them away. "Get back to your party, shows over."

"Figures you'd get the pretty girl," Sam teased.

Zak gave Sam a wide grin then shifted his attention back to Vixin. He scooted his chair closer, wrapping one around over her shoulder.

Vixin couldn't look at him. Her heart raced as if she'd just run an entire marathon. She wasn't even sure she'd have the voice to speak.

"Want to get some air?"

She nodded and Zak took her hand and led her toward the door. Their friends whooped and hollered, but Zak's only response was a vulgar gesture before they slipped from the room.

"Don't let them bother you."

She finally laughed. "Did you forget who you're talking to? A month ago, they were all terrified of me."

Zak pulled her close. "I never was." He leaned down to kiss her again and the knot in her stomach tightened. She couldn't get enough of him. Couldn't get close enough, but when his fingertips lifted the edge of her shirt she pulled back.

"Don't worry, I won't take advantage of you."

She smirked against his lips. "As if you could."

His warm hands traced over her bare back, eliciting further sensations that made her lose all sense of time.

True to his word, Zak made no further advances and it was he who finally broke their kiss. Breathless, he pressed his forehead against hers. "Weeks ago, you would have twisted my arm for that."

"Weeks ago, I would have broken your arm for that. Maybe both."

He placed a soft kiss on her forehead. "No matter how shitty this world gets, I'll never regret coming here. Not after meeting you."

"Dad says all things happen for a reason."

He smirked and pressed another long kiss to her lips. "Come on, let's get back inside before their imaginations run wild."

They celebrated for hours, teasing the new couple before returning to their merriment. She didn't mind. It felt nice to belong, to be teased and picked on without them fearing her.

Zak kept one arm around her shoulder, and she wondered what her father would think of him.

"Where are you from?" she asked.

"Montana. And you?"

"Tennessee at the moment."

"At the moment?"

"Dad likes to travel."

"Well, when we get back it looks like I'm moving to Tennessee."

"You'd do that? Leave your family?"

He shrugged. "I have three older brothers. And both of my parents are alive. I have to leave the nest sometime."

She smiled. "We haven't been to Montana in a while. Dad likes it there. Why leave your family when I can simply bring mine along?"

Zak stiffened. "So I'll have to meet your dad."

"You sound scared."

"After dealing with you shouldn't I be? Any tips?"

She smirked. "Don't back down."

The music stopped and many simply plopped down on the floor rather than return to their rooms. She lazed against Zak, about to turn in herself when the door crashed open.

Fire erupted from all sides and Vixin reached for a blade that wasn't there. Zak tackled them both to the ground and shielded her from the shards of ice racing through the air. They struck the wood behind their heads, sinking deep.

Vixin raised her head in time to see Anton's body fall limp. Blood pooled around him and then another fell. More blood. And then another.

Vixin's cry of rage shattered the night and her magic erupted with it. Unfamiliar faces poured inside the room and Vixin let the greenery run wild, snaking around anyone who dared enter.

Zak lunged to her front, blocking an attack that had blood pouring from his forearm. She shattered the wooden floor, impaling his attackers before shoving them from the balcony. Vixin dove for a weapon they'd dropped and kicked another to Zak.

Vixin jumped through the broken doorway to assess their situation and her stomach dropped.

Everything was on fire. Everything they'd worked so hard to build, all their dreams falling. Fading.

A body slammed into hers and Vixin tumbled over the railing. Her magic flew out from the surrounding trees to slow her descent, but she still cried out upon hitting the ground. Pain radiated up her knees, but Vixin didn't stop slashing.

Every last one. She'd kill every last one of them.

Vixin took a breath and launched herself into the fray. She didn't care how many there were. Didn't care what kind of magic they possessed. All she knew was duck, swing, pivot. A dance she'd been learning since she was a child.

Vixin ducked behind a tree to escape a barrage of flames and took off into the woods. Let them follow her into her domain, where every living thing was a weapon at her disposal.

She pierced the heart of the first to catch up to her and then tore through the knee of the second. Vixin continued circling, searching. She'd left Zak on the platform. She needed to get back to—

Wind ripped at her clothes and Vixin spun, already tugging at her vines. They didn't respond. She tugged again, but some invisible force kept them at bay. Real fear clawed its way through her body, choking her with its hold.

This was it. This was all she had.

Someone grabbed her wrist and ice shot through those surrounding her. Zak didn't give them a passing glance as he raced through the woods, weaving in and out of trees.

He skidded to a sudden halt, threw open a door, and shoved her inside before jumping in after.

"Cover the door!"

"What are you doing?"

Zak grabbed her face with both hands, but she couldn't see him in the dark. "Cover the door. Right now."

Vixin fought past her tears and obeyed, lacing as much greenery over the door as she could. Over a hiding place she'd known nothing about.

"Why—"

Zak clamped a hand over her mouth and heavy footsteps sounded above. She didn't dare breathe as they trotted back and forth, shouting orders.

A single voice screamed for help but was silenced before she could even think about assisting. She was out of energy anyway. If they found the door, that was it.

Vixin struggled to keep her breathing steady. Why? Why send so many after one little band of thieves and for what? A few weapons?

Zak took a shuddering breath and shifted so his body wasn't on top of hers. "Are you hurt?" he asked.

"No. You?" He didn't respond so Vixin assumed he'd shaken his head. "Where are the others hiding? I might be able to tunnel to them."

Silence.

"Zak?" She touched his arm only to find him shaking. "What's wrong?" Vixin felt his face and the tears streaming down it. "Zak?"

"They're gone."

"Whose gone?"

He gritted his teeth and a sob tore through his body. "Everyone. They're all gone."

What? No, that wasn't possible.

"Zak, where's Sam?"

Zak let out a strangled cry at his friend's name and something in her gut wrenched. It crushed her, pressing a weight so hard over her chest she wasn't sure she'd ever breathe again. But she did, and the shards of grief dug deeper.

They were gone. In the blink of an eye. Gone.

Vixin wrapped her arms around Zak and he clutched her middle, sobbing into her shirt. She tried to hold it together, but no amount of training could have prepared her for this. For the crushing pain of death.

Zak had made her a part of his family. And losing family hurt far worse than any wound she'd ever experienced.

Zak eventually separated himself from her and fell asleep in the corner. She must have fallen asleep too because the next time her eyes opened, she was freezing.

Vixin cocked her head to the side, trying to listen for any signs of movement. Her and Zak couldn't hide forever.

She shifted the dirt with her magic and daylight greeted her through a small hole. Vixin took another moment to listen before widening the hole enough to poke her head out.

Nothing moved.

"Zak," she whispered. "I think they're gone." Vixin shifted the plants away from the door and shoved it open. Afternoon sun blinded her for several seconds, but she climbed out anyway. "Come on, we have to get moving."

She surveyed the area, her heart breaking at the sight of smoke rising from their home. Part of the structure had collapsed but she tried not to think about who might be buried beneath.

Vixin jumped back into the hole. "Zak, we have to—"

She froze. The world faded and some small part of her that'd been barely holding it together shattered into a million little pieces.

"Zak?" Her voice broke, her entire world breaking with it.

She crawled across the small space and touched his hand only to recoil at the feel of his icy skin. Her lips parted and a noise she didn't recognize escaped her lips.

Vixin tried to breathe. She wrestled with her lungs, fighting, and finally screamed.

Memories flooded blurry vision. The first time they'd met while running through the woods. The first time she'd gone on a mission with him and his friends. Their first training session. Her first kiss.

Vixin's jaw clenched and unclenched, her breathing rapid and shallow as an entirely new kind of pain lanced through her core.

Why?

Why?

Why?

She screamed the word, staring toward the heavens for some kind of answer.

She'd wasted time. So much precious time. If anyone knew what survival meant. What the consequences of failure were...

Vixin took a shuddering breath only to have another jolt of pain tighten around her chest.

Last night. That's all she'd had with him. One night.

She balled her fists and curled in on herself, clutching her heart as if she could hold the pieces together. Vixin pressed her forehead to the ground and sob after sob tore through her tired body.

She didn't know how long she stayed that way. She didn't care.

Her breathing slowed and her chest loosened ever so slightly.

Vixin lifted her head to look at him, her eyes drifting to the blood on his shirt and wound in his stomach. If she'd had enough light, if she'd known, she might have been able to find Sam before—

They're all dead.

Vixin drew her knees into her chest and let the silence of the world take over. Why was she left behind? Why was she the only one who—more tears fell, but after what seemed like an eternity, Vixin struggled to her feet.

She stared at Zak. At the boy she'd tried to push away. At the boy who'd never given up.

With an aching heart, Vixin crawled from the cellar. She stood at its edge and finally called upon the wisteria to cover his body. It crawled over the wound first and then lilies bloomed, followed by roses and fauna.

She wouldn't bury him in the place he feared. She'd let him sit in the sun, lost within a field of flowers that no one would ever disturb.

She took a breath and turned toward their damaged home. Or what was left of it. Vixin took a step forward, followed by another, unable to tear her gaze away. Fires had torn the base from its branches and smoke still rose as a reminder of the carnage.

She trudged toward it anyway, unable to stop herself even after seeing the first body.

An empty face. Another contorted in a scream. Then—

Vixin choked out a sob and hit her knees all over again. Sam.

Grief consumed her, tearing every bit of self-control from her grasp as she howled in sorrow and rage.

She clenched her teeth, biting the inside of her cheek and that depthless sorrow shifted to burning rage. She clawed at the ground then lifted her head in the direction of her enemy's camp.

Vixin placed one foot beneath her body and rose. Bloody. Aching. But far from broken.

Oh, so very far.

They'd pay. Every. Single. One.

Vixin wiped her tears and tried to ignore the faces as she lifted herself toward a section on the second floor. The section where her and Zak's rooms sat side by side.

His was half charred but hers sat untouched. As if it'd been unworthy to join its neighbors in death.

She lifted herself through the window and went straight for her weapons. The knives she strapped to her back. Two shorter blades went in her boots and she strapped a third around her waist for good measure.

Vixin didn't bother changing her bloody clothes. She'd wear them until she got her revenge and if she died in them, then so be it.

Vixin exited and paused to survey the carnage below. She pulled at her magic and let the Wisteria grow, weaving between the bodies of her fallen comrades as she lowered herself to the ground.

She poured magic from her body, feeding, feeding, feeding until the sharp sting of physical pain begged her to stop.

But she didn't. Couldn't. Vixin took several steps back and let the poisonous ones take root, springing to life among the beauty. They crawled and weaved, hiding the destruction that had shattered her newfound life.

Vixin staggered back, leaned against the nearest tree, and slid to the ground. Tears rolled down her face in a river she wasn't sure would ever stop. She just sat there, staring at the beautifully haunted place that would forever hold a piece of her fractured heart.

13

THE GIRL AND HER REVENGE

Vixin followed the same path her and Zak had trekked days ago. Only this time it was empty. Hollow. Replaced by an unending rage that crackled through her in waves.

Vixin curled against a tree and pulled her cloak tight as the rain started again. She didn't bother with a canopy. Instead, she let the water soak through her clothes until her body felt the same as her heart. Numb. At least in the moments the rage receded.

Vixin dozed, letting the monster her magic had become slumber. Rest. Recover. Because when she unleashed it again, she wasn't letting a single person walk out of that camp alive.

The days drifted as she walked and Vixin let herself relive the memories. Her magic shifted and pulled, digging beneath her skin, craving release. But she held it back and when that wall came into view, her memories faded, replaced by a lust for their blood.

Nothing made sense. Why slaughter a small camp for stealing a few weapons? It wasn't like they'd hurt anyone.

Vixin clenched her fists. Her heart pounded in her chest as their hollow faces flashed in her mind's eye.

She climbed a tree, keeping her magic on a tight leash as she examined the men guarding the wall. They smiled at one another, passing drinks and food between them as if they hadn't just murdered over thirty people a few days ago.

No shame. No remorse.

Vixin took a calming breath. Death didn't matter, as long as she made each of them pay for what they'd done. She'd shatter the night and make each of them regret ever setting foot outside their fortress.

She slid from the tree and stalked the perimeter until nightfall. Vixin counted the guards, located the barracks, and took a mental note of those with long range weapons. She was certain all the guards had some sort of magic.

Vixin spent the day shifting her plants into place far beneath their feet. The soil was thicker the further down she went, but with so many enemies she needed this to play out perfectly. For Sam and Zak. For Anton and Blitz and Daniel.

Night descended and Vixin slipped from a tree. She checked her weapons and stretched her stiff body. Now was the moment to make her father proud. Despite his reluctance to speak of his military life, he had told her a few stories about his friends. About those he'd lost, those who'd saved him, and those he missed dearly.

She understood now. He'd never wanted her to fall among the lost. He wanted her to find people to spend her life with, people that would gift her with treasured memories.

She'd found that and these monsters had torn it away.

Vixin dashed between the trees and lifted herself over the wall on silent feet. No one saw her slip inside. She pressed her back against the nearest wall then poured her magic through the earth, harnessing hundreds of seeds she'd put into place that afternoon. They rose another foot to the surface.

No alarm sounded.

Vixin made her way through the compound, keeping to the shadows, until she reached the center building. The same one her and Zak had spent a single night in. She wanted to personally kill whoever had given the order before she unleashed hell upon the others.

Vixin reached for the seeds and raised them another foot. Then another. She listened, waiting to see if anyone with similar abilities would notice, but the silence stretched.

Vixin pulled her hood up and slipped in through the back door. Warmth from the ovens greeted her, singing her wet skin, but Vixin ignored it and crawled toward the voices. She narrowly avoided a young woman working the kitchens and refused to look at the girl's face.

Vixin crouched in the doorway to listen.

"You should have seen it. The place looked like a damn treehouse."

"Was it the right group this time?"

"You saw the tunnel he made from our warehouse. Earth, just like the rumors claim."

Vixin's hand shook as she snaked her magic in through the backdoor.

Another voice spoke. "Based upon the descriptions we received, I'd say the boy was a bit young."

"Descriptions from people scared out of their minds."

Another to his left chimed in. "Even if it wasn't them, we still eliminated a threat. They were thieves and living far too close for my comfort."

"We shouldn't tell Atilla until we know for sure."

Their voices faded. Earth. Zak was dead because—her body shook—because of her magic. Because they thought he was someone he wasn't.

It'd been her idea to sneak in. Her idea to tell them he possessed her magic. Her breathing accelerated and Vixin clenched her chest. She had to calm down. Calm down. Breathe.

Vixin peeked around the corner and studied the chairs. Only five of them.

She wiped her stinging eyes, drew her long knives, and sprinted through the doorway, plunging her blade straight through the nearest man's back. Vixin yanked it out and lunged at the man to his right, slitting his throat in one swift movement.

She eyed the others and tugged at her magic. Nothing. Vixin growled and tugged again, but it felt as though an invisible wall had blocked it off. Just like before.

Something collided with the back of her head and stars shot across her vision as she hit the floor. One of her knives slid across the room, but she kept the other clutched in one hand. Vixin swung wildly, cutting nothing but thin air as she stumbled to her feet and backed against the wall.

She pulled at the magic again, but that invisible wall stood firm, blocking her from the very things that were going to tear this place down.

Dizzy, but raging, Vixin took a quick head count. Three stood in quiet concentration while four others edged away from the corner of the room.

One's mouth gaped. "It's a girl."

"I'm not blind you moron."

"But if this girl is the one using earth magic, then we didn't get the one responsible for—"

"Shut up," another voice boomed. "Girl or no, she stole from us and we can't allow that." He stomped toward her and leaned forward. "You're not the only one who can play with magic. Where I come from, thieves are punished. Severely."

She didn't speak, couldn't, with the rage bubbling beneath the surface. They had her magic pinned, so what? She'd trained for years without it.

He smiled as if she still didn't have a blade in one hand and just as he tried to speak again, Vixin yanked the knife from her boot and shoved it into his throat.

He spluttered, grasping at the blade. The wall restraining her magic wavered and Vixin dove through that tiny crack, grasping a vine before ripping it from the ground. It wrapped around one of the men lost in concentration and the poisonous thorns pierced his arm.

He winced, took a few steps back, and cursed. The invisible wall thickened again.

A hulking man in the corner drew a small knife and greenery that didn't belong to her ripped from the floorboards. The vines engulfed her body, tying it down. Vixin fought, screamed, and kicked, but the vines forced her to drop her weapon and fall to her knees.

"I apologize, but it has to be done." He took several steps closer, confident she couldn't lash out at him again. He knelt before her and Vixin lunged, sinking her teeth into his neck.

He screeched and the knife in his hand plunged into her side, withdrew, and plunged in again. Tears stung the corners of her eyes, but something in the barrier faltered again and Vixin dove for it. She grabbed the seedlings she'd planted and shattered the rest of the wooden floor.

They scrambled, desperate, and Vixin breathed in their fear. Fed from it. The greenery caught each individual one by one and squeezed the life from their bodies.

She took a step, but blinding pain lanced through her side. Vixin pressed a hand to the wounds and it came away bloody. She cursed, kicked the dead body nearest to her and climbed the stairs.

Vines stretched out on all sides, slithering beneath doors for those who would wake, only to step on her deadly thorns. She almost wished she could be there to witness each and every death.

Vixin stormed through an empty room and climbed out the window. Pain tore through her side again as she lifted herself onto the roof, but the pain in her heart cut deeper.

There were already people below, running to sound the alarm. Good, let them be scared.

Vixin planted her feet and fed her magic through the ground. She summoned all the seeds and plants she'd shifted into place then let the world erupt.

Those at the gates recoiled, many jumping inside the safety of the walls as plants crawled over, under, and around. They engulfed the buildings, tearing through structures one by one. People screamed, running from the terror, but they couldn't escape her poisonous barbs.

Guards rushed out, shouting orders that would never be obeyed. They ran, many cutting through her plants with magic of their own. But their bodies turned sluggish and their magic flickered out as they grasped at their throats and choked in their own blood.

She wouldn't give them the mercy of a swift death.

The cries of alarm slowly faded as more and more people fell into a painful slumber. And when crickets and the sounds of the night were the only things left, Vixin finally let her magic fade.

She collapsed on the rooftop and another wave of pain that had nothing to do with the wounds in her side assaulted her body. Tears rolled down her face as she gazed out onto the green carnage. She hadn't let anyone out. Didn't care who they were, only that her friends were avenged.

Despite her body's protest, Vixin used her magic to lift herself from rooftop to rooftop, careful of the poison she'd left behind.

She set herself outside the gate and leaned against the nearest tree, letting grief finally take its toll.

VIXIN'S EYES fluttered open with the first rays of dawn. She shifted and hissed at the pain in her side. The blood had stopped, which meant her wounds probably weren't that serious. She half laughed to herself. Lucky or cursed, she wasn't sure.

Maybe she'd been allowed to live because she still had someone to hunt down. This Atilla. She glanced toward the camp. Eventually, someone would come along and see what she'd done. They'd report back to him and simply knowing he'd fear for his life was enough to satisfy her for now.

Footsteps echoed down the road and Vixin struggled to her feet. She wouldn't hide. If it were more men who called this place home, she'd gladly let them go in.

Vixin pressed a hand into her side feeling the trickle of blood again. She'd have to stitch it later, but for now, she waited.

The procession, consisting of at least fifty men, halted several yards away. They seemed to study her before two men separated from the group and approached. Vixin held her ground, the magic already writhing beneath her feet. She didn't care who noticed.

They stopped, gazed at the carnage behind her, and then one spoke. "Did you do this?"

"Does it matter?" she snapped. Vixin noted the way he kept his hands at his side, though his companion didn't do the same.

He gave her a sideways grin. "Looks like you did our work for us." He furrowed his brow. "Though I guess there's no looting whatever's inside."

"Not unless you want to die."

They stood in awkward silence, but Vixin still didn't release the hold on her magic.

"Are you alone?" he asked. When she didn't respond he waved a hand toward his companions. "You could join us if you wanted."

Vixin snorted. "Not a chance. And if you don't want to end up like them, you'll get out of my way."

He raised his hands and took a step to the side. She noted the bracelet around his wrist. The same color as her own.

Vixin stormed past, but his companion protested. "Reece, she's just a kid."

"She can take care of herself."

Vixin didn't look back. He knew what crawled beneath her feet. The kind of hell she could still unleash if any of them came after her.

When she could no longer see them in the distance, her shoulders shook, but Vixin held her head high. Despite the devastation. Despite the scars, she'd loved, and she could honestly say that loving and losing was far better than never having loved at all.

She'd had something most spent their entire lives searching for and she'd cherish every memory.

She'd cherish her friends.

She'd cherish her family.

She'd cherish Zak.

ACKNOWLEDGMENTS

First, I want to thank my readers who make this whole writing journey worthwhile. Without your constant motivation and support, I wouldn't have gotten this far. Seeing your reactions and receiving your excited messages about my work has really spurred me forward into making this a lifelong career. I hope you enjoyed this installment, even if you did shed a few tears, and I hope you'll continue following along with my characters as they continue their epic journey.

Next, I want to thank my family, namely my little sister and husband, who both support me day in and day out. Mandy, I promise I'll finish all the stories I've told you about, though I can't promise I'll write as fast as you can devour them. Kyle, you've been the most supportive person I could ever ask for in my life. All those nights of watching TV while I silently pecked away at my laptop will be worth it in the long run. Thank you.

And lastly, to those who have read my work and provided incredible feedback, thank you so very much. Every comment gives an author insight into their book that they might not have otherwise come up with and sometimes it shapes things into being that we wouldn't have written before.

To everyone: Always follow your dreams, no matter how distant they may seem.

ABOUT THE AUTHOR

J.E. Reed is the Multi-award-winning author of the Chronopoint Chronicles and lives in Cincinnati, Ohio with her husband and cats. Reed always had an interest in writing but didn't explore that talent fully until 2015 when the idea for her first novel, *Running with the Wolves*, crept through her imagination and demanded to be written. Reed owns her own business as a Licensed Massage Therapist and spends her downtime swimming, hiking, and tackling the occasional mud run with friends.

Visit her webpage at jereedbooks.com

CPSIA information can be obtained
at www.ICGtesting.com
Printed in the USA
FSHW011549171020
74837FS